CHARLES BOYLE has published a number of poetry collections (for which he was shortlisted for the T.S. Eliot, Forward and Whitbread Prizes), a short novel (winner of the 2008 McKitterick Prize) and two books combining text and photography. He runs the small press CB editions. This is his first book of stories.

CHARLES BOYLE
The Manet Girl

SALT

CROMER

PUBLISHED BY SALT PUBLISHING
12 Norwich Road, Cromer, Norfolk NR27 0AX United Kingdom

First published by Salt Publishing, 2013

Printed in Great Britain by Clays Ltd, St Ives plc

Typeset in Paperback 9.5/13

ISBN 978 1 907773 45 7 paperback

1 3 5 7 9 8 6 4 2

CONTENTS

I for my part have never been able to understand his figures nor, for all my asking, have I ever found anyone who does. In these frescoes one sees, in various attitudes, a man in one place, a woman standing in another, one figure accompanied by the head of a lion, another by an angel in the guise of a cupid; and heaven knows what it all means.

– Vasari, *Lives of the Artists*, on Giorgione

The Manet Girl

BUDAPEST

In the kitchen, which is the room where they eat, an ancient peasant cat, no fancy breed, is lying awkwardly on a chair and panting, though the day is cold. No one is paying it attention. Beyond the window are clouds, fields, the kind of view people call uninterrupted.

He is trespassing, he has no right to be here, and it feels like freedom.

'The wood across the valley is the largest in the county,' James announces from the other end of the table, as if he had planted every tree himself.

'There are wolves,' C says quietly, looking at him, teasing.

'They bay to the moon,' he says.

'They do more than that.'

'Is it OK?' asks the woman called Marcia. 'Should we get it some water or something?'

She's worrying about the cat, and he is wary of the drift. If anyone asks if he has animals of his own, he'll say no. He has no affinity with dumb creatures. And yet just this week he has yielded to pressure – family pressure, normality pressure: he was cornered – and purchased a pair of rabbits for his pair of children. They squat, shivering with fear, or hunger. How is he to know? Their droppings are hard brown beads.

The cat is ill. It is a fuse easily lit, after so much wine and loosening of voices. James, C's husband, is intent on spending a large amount of money on an operation to prolong its life. Let it go, C says, as if pushing it to the side of her plate. Anything else is selfishness, not love. He wants to spend that money for himself, truth be told. Take the cat in and bring it back hurt, bewildered, pawing at its shaved and mangled body, or take it in unknowing and put it down. A good life come to term, and no suffering. *That* is mercy.

He knows it is her marriage she is talking about. Everything here – the hand-painted plates on the dresser, the photographs, the scribbled lists and numbers of emergency plumbers – is a stage set, history, disposable. Excitement makes him tremble. He wants to turn to whoever is sitting next to him, which happens to be Marcia, and hug her. He knows that if anyone says even the weakest thing funny, he is danger of laughing too loud.

'I'm sorry,' C says, standing up. Lighter than skin, the folds of her dress cascade; he still has the ghost of it on his fingers from when they came in. She has, he's noticed, a way of widening her eyes after speaking; she is not apologising at all. 'Really, you shouldn't be listening to this. Who wants more wine?'

Marcia puts her hand over the rim of her glass, as if she's about to perform a conjuring trick. But James does want, pushing his own glass across the table. The gambling table: *faites vos jeux*. It occurs to him that James has him down as gay. There were meant to be just four around the table, C and James and Marcia and his brother, Maurice, recently widowed, whom she'd wanted to put together with

Marcia, but when she called and his brother had explained that he happened to be staying then of course, why not.

Marcia is a counsellor, with devout opinions. Everything can be explained. Everyone else, to her, is like a pet, dependent. James is a retired lawyer, a former colleague of his brother's; he is, or was, a brilliant mind, his brother has said. C is his fate. A few weeks from now – sooner, sooner – she will turn to him in bed, and say: 'James thought you were gay.' He is sure of this. Her hand will be toying with him, she will be everything he has waited for.

'Did *you*?'

'He still does.'

~

Across the street, Marcia is coming out of the village bookshop with Maurice. She turns away, but they have seen her. There is a pause, until the road is clear, and then they are surrounding her with their togetherness, thanking her for the lunch, fumbling with bags, showing her what they have bought in the bookshop. She is not surprised.

Maurice has sprained his wrist. He parades his bandage. He was putting the lawnmower back in the shed; he slipped, he fell, he put out a hand to save himself, and now this. For all that he is a lawyer, it's a wonder he didn't electrocute himself too. Men are so helpless. He can't even work a tin-opener. Marcia is cooking for him.

'He did everything, for years and years,' Marcia says. She means for Alice, Maurice's wife, who is dead, who died of complications. Alice was alcoholic, everyone knows this.

'And really, it's bloody difficult,' Marcia goes on. She is gleeful, victorious. 'He's so stubborn. He's given so much he's forgotten how to take. It's the harder thing, of course, but just as important. We're starting from scratch.'

3

She has known Marcia for a decade, longer. She is happy for her. She hadn't conceived that life could be so simple.

'She's a good teacher,' says Maurice, a schoolboyish gleam in his eyes that takes her aback. He likes his food.

The eyes, yes, and other small things too – the way he tilts his head to the left when he's listening – though there is little obvious physical resemblance between the brothers, nothing you'd notice at first glance. She suspects that they get on but they are not close, these brothers. They see things in each other that they don't like about themselves, they are happy to stay out of range. Brotherhood: the roles assumed, the competition, one pitching camp where the other leaves space unguarded.

Maurice is still looking at her, awaiting a blessing.

She is beginning to think like Marcia, to analyse, which is a form of helplessness. She looks over Maurice's shoulder: the street, the weathered stone buildings, the shopkeepers who chat and ask neutral questions and tot up little sums; and then the green hills, as still as on the picture postcards. The names on the village war memorial – Atkinson, Hancock, Smith, Weatherspoon – are a mantra that holds this place in its grip. She met Alice only twice, maybe three times. Once at a law society dinner. There had been a point at which she'd been completely beautiful. Her glance was withering. It was a long marriage; there are children somewhere, out in the world, Hong Kong, Australia. The weather is mild, changeable. At the weekend it will be hot. The traffic on this street gets worse every year. Marcia and Maurice head off towards the post office, her hand cupping his elbow.

She has a flat in town – really it is her husband's flat, James's, there are law books in glass-fronted bookcases, but since he retired it's almost never used. He wakes in her bed to the sound of shouting voices and the screech of tyres. A fight in the street, he thinks. Grey light, sometime around dawn. Naked, he walks through to the living room and finds her sitting cross-legged on the floor, watching a film on TV. He strokes her hair. Leaning back into his shoulder, she pats the floor for him sit beside beside her. Together they watch two women driving fast through small towns, on the run. She will watch to the end, even though the end is foretold by the music. After half an hour, with the heating still not come on, he sweeps the covering from the sofa and wraps it around them.

Daily, the world reveals more of itself. Sometimes he feels like a tourist in his own city. He talks to strangers. He tells her about the man he met while walking through the park, a man like a gypsy with his hair twisted around the strap at the back of his baseball cap. The man said he was from the north of Sweden, the far north, and he was a poet – would he like to hear a poem? He said he would rather hear a joke. The man told him a long joke, it must have gone on for at least five minutes, entirely in Swedish or some remote dialect from beyond the Arctic Circle, and by the end the man was doubled up, laughing uncontrol-lably. She laughs too, not just with her face but her toes, her fingers, her belly.

Or he is waiting at the barrier when the train comes in and does its meek slow stop and the doors open and the people file through, the busy ones checking their watches and the old women who have been travelling since the days of porters and the students with their crass but ergonomic backpacks, and he carries on waiting till the platform is bare as a seaside promenade in winter and she isn't there. What she teaches her lovers, he thinks, and not for the first time, is patience.

There are days when there's white cloud all morning and mizzly rain in the afternoon and then at seven in the evening the sky clears to china blue and the sun shines undimmed as if it's never put a foot wrong in its life.

Not patience of the kind that's deemed a virtue (it isn't). There've been times when, heading to her flat, they haven't been able to wait but have ducked into an alleyway and torn at each other's clothing.

He goes home. It would fit better if when he comes in his wife is peeling carrots but she isn't, she's just standing in the kitchen knowing there is a next thing to do but having lost track.

'Did you get the . . . ?' she asks.

'The milk?'

'The milk, yes. We're out.'

'I forgot,' he says. 'I'm sorry.'

From his room at the top of the house where he now sleeps he can see the rabbit cage in the garden, and his younger child sitting cross-legged in front of it. No sign of the rabbits. They are in their hutch, their little room, sulking.

He phones her. He doesn't leave a message.

On the way to the station, he decides, she came across a maimed owl, which needed putting back in one piece. Or just as she was about to leave a friend called her from Romania, or maybe Hungary – which country is Budapest the capital of? – in tears. She has a problem with time-tables, with the 24-hour clock. She doesn't wear a watch. Her appetite is limitless and like most people with appetite she is also generous. When he pulls on clothes and says he must go she kicks off the sheets and opens her legs, offering, asking to be kissed, lips to lips.

He is late, so often these days, but his son is still there, cross-legged, in front of the rabbits' cage, waiting for them to appear. All day, all night if need be. Where it comes from, this stubbornness, this dedication, he has no idea. He cannot recall when he has been more proud. If this is his son, he cannot be all that bad: this a way, one of many he knows, of damning himself.

The rabbits, he thinks, have been eaten by a fox – there are plenty around, probably more than where she is, in the countryside – but there is no litter of tufts of fur and bloody scraps. Or they have escaped, are returning to the wild, in which case they will not survive for long.

His phone rings. She tells him she's tired, that today has not been the best of days, that –

'When will I see you?'

She's not sure – the weekend, maybe. She'll come up on Saturday, yes. Saturday early.

'The milk train?' he says. Then he asks after the cat.

There is no cat. The cat disappeared, she says, weeks ago. She has heard of this before: they have some instinct that tells them their time is drawing near, and they go off alone to meet their maker in private.

When he looks out of the window again his son is not there but the rabbits are, out of their hutch and pressed up against the wire. He closes his eyes and sees the wood across the valley, 'the largest in the county'; he enters its shade, its darkness, hears rustlings and flutterings and sudden sharp cries. Though they have done nothing to deserve it – but when was anything decided on merit? – animals have the last word, even the last laugh. They are primed for this, it's in their genetic engineering. The

7

thought is like a mouthful of food that tastes very different from what you'd expected, from what you'd imagined.

~

A year later C is in Budapest, visiting Hannah. Hand-luggage only, and she still doesn't wear a watch. Instead, on her wrist there is a sequence of numbers, written in biro and starting to smudge. It is a cold afternoon, autumn, but they are eating outside, on a terrace. Life is complicated. Also with them, but not just now at the table, is a Peruvian child, a boy of around six, with flat black hair and eyes so clear and deep she could swim in them.

'Oh, him,' she says, in answer to something Hannah has said. *Him*, in distinction from the other him, James, whom they've been talking about for the past half hour. It's like being part of a reading group, discussing the characters.

She is holding a stuffed animal, a sheep, which the boy has more than relinquished. He is over there, crouched in a corner of the terrace, exploring. They have been swimming in the pool of an old and expensive hotel that predates the Communist era and has come out the other side with surly changing-room attendants untrained in the ways of customer service. She feels lucky to have all her life been free.

Except that she is not free. She feels she is on the set of a film, whether farce or thriller she doesn't yet know. The boy is the adopted child of Hannah and her Hungarian husband; the husband has been cast adrift by Hannah but is determined to climb back on board and has taken to following them around, stalking them. He refuses to drown. Hence the numbers inked on her hand, which she must punch into the alarm system in Hannah's apartment within ten seconds of entering. She scrabbles around in the dark, trying not to panic, imagining that she will be arrested and taken to an underground cellar and interrogated under a blinding light and will have her fingernails slowly pulled out.

'He has wonderful eyes,' she says. And adds, having given herself the cue: 'He has a wonderful cock. Effervescent.'

The boy comes to his mother with a spider cupped in his hands. 'A boy spider or a girl spider?' he wants to know. He speaks English like an American. (This, she has been meaning to say, is why Hannah cannot leave him alone in the apartment while she's at work, alone with the TV tuned to American game-shows; and why she herself cannot abide indoors for more than an hour in that clean, functional but badly windowed flat, where you have to switch on a light even to make breakfast; why she must take the boy out and thereby condemn herself to the frantic punching of the code on the keypad when they have run out of things to do. But she has only been here for two days.)

'For god's sake,' Hannah says, laughing. She is happy, or believes she is. She delivers a lecture on the good life – Hannah is not unlike Marcia, in her belief that life can be made to fit – while all the time attending to the boy's asking, asking. Why do spiders have so many legs? How long do spiders live? Is this a baby spider or a grown-up?

The couple at the next table are tourists, like herself. German, Dutch? The man is intent on the map at the back of his guidebook, folded out on the table. The woman is looking across the river, so entranced she appears to have forgotten what it is she should be doing with the forkful of food she has raised. Should she put it back on her plate? Or into her body? If so, through which opening?

Now a man is walking towards them: the waiter, or a secret policeman, or Hannah's outcast, desperate husband.

C really doesn't mind which. She sips wine; it's not for her to say. She looks beyond the man to where the woman at the next table is looking, across the river sparkling in the afternoon sunshine.

OK, the boy says, but how does it *know* it's grown up, why doesn't it just keep on growing more legs?

Sometimes in old films the camera pulls back from the intimate – the kiss, the fight, the horses being saddled – to show the backdrop panorama: the cityscape, its domes and spires and palaces, the snow-capped mountains. How beautiful, you think. And then just as you begin to suspect that it's not for real, that it's a painted backdrop, they cut to the next scene. The budget was tight, you can understand this, it wouldn't stretch to a whole crew staying for months in a luxury scenic location. You can forgive, if there's anything to be forgiven, which there isn't. But not too tight for a painter to paint that landscape, with all the hours of research and the patience of each brushstroke, even though it will be on screen for barely more than a second.

THE MANET GIRL

The girl in the café had a bandage on her hand, extending over the wrist. RSI, she told him – from making too many coffees, though this seemed unlikely to Robert. The most customers he'd ever seen in that café was two women, one child either asleep or yowling for a Coke float, and a man pretending to write a novel on his laptop while nursing a single espresso for half the morning. And there were two girls to serve them, this one and the one he'd heard called Penny, the one with her hair tied back with a rubber band. He'd masturbated more times than this girl had made coffee, and *he* didn't have RSI.

Agreed the place wasn't busy, but she'd been making coffee, day in, day out, for four years.

He tried to cheer her up.

'You know Manet? The woman at the bar in the Folies-Bergère?'

There was a bowl of fruit near the cash till. He took three oranges and placed them just to her left. The girl called Penny glanced over, as if he might be stealing them.

She rested her hands on the edge of the worktop and looked glum. This wasn't a long way from how she usually looked. He understood that she didn't want to be here at all, but where else? The worktop was a little too high but she knew who Robert was talking about, both the painter and the girl.

'At the time he painted that, he had tertiary syphilis,' he told her. 'Then he got gangrene and had a leg amputated. Then he died.'

'Did he have RSI?' she asked.

Do painters get RSI? House painters, probably yes: the same strokes again and again, brush or roller. Art painters, except for the ones who just do stripes, probably not. They take longer breaks, they mix up the strokes. Some of them employ assistants to do the dots or the straight up-and-down work for them.

Imogen knew more about the subject than Robert. She had been to art college. Had she painted more paintings than she had made cups of coffee? She shrugged, not with her shoulders but her eyes, which met his and then glanced away. She hadn't counted. And now, looking back, she saw them as a kind of winter soup, a thick broth, served cold. She had left all her work behind at the college, and ignored the letters that told her they would be destroyed if she didn't collect them. She was free.

He said she could still be an artist if she wanted – she could be an artist in the way that actors he knew were actors. Most of them worked in wine bars.

And then, on a whim – because the sun was shining, because there was no one else in the café except Penny and the man in the corner at the back who may or may not have been writing a book, and because he was showing off – he said that he'd commission a painting from her.

She laughed. 'A painting of what?'

Anything she wanted, and he'd buy it. Five hundred pounds. She guessed that he had no more than ten in his wallet, and she was right.

She tilted her head. Manet's bar girl had her head tilted too, just slightly. Her hair was cut in an uneven fringe – badly cut, she'd probably done it herself in front of the bathroom mirror – and she was a bit pale and slightly heavy around the thighs but nothing he'd want to criticise, especially as she spent most of every day surrounded by food.

'No strings,' he added, shaking his head, knowing as he said it that there *was* something sexual about spending money like this. Not that he fancied her. She was a girl with a downturned mouth he wanted to make smile, was all. This was just a market transaction, seller and buyer, supply and demand.

She looked in two worlds. Had she even heard what he'd said? It occurred to Robert that she was about to break into tears. As he moved the oranges back into their bowl one spilled from his hands and rolled beneath a table.

'Manet painted prostitutes,' she said. She was perfectly composed. 'The painter of modern life' – she was quoting from somewhere.

'I didn't –'

'I know. But –' She held up her bandaged hand. Using her other hand she could still, just about, work the coffee machine. But even if she had canvas, materials, studio, she wasn't up to painting.

'Still, you need a break. It's just going to get worse, like this.'

~

They had things in common. They both knew people who really were artists – not famous, no one the other might have heard of, but people who spent their days in unheated studios in derelict warehouses, pottering about, priming their canvases, making their marks and then overpainting and making them again. They both had uncles who had died. Somewhere between them was the average age at which you are alive when your uncle dies. They disliked the same films – which isn't the same as liking the same films, Robert knew that, but some days after talking with Imogen he called the artist he knew who'd once done a drawing he remembered and which now he had to have, because he thought Imogen might like it too. What had happened to that drawing? The artist told him it had been done for a project; there were many artists involved and they had all made drawings which they rolled up and put in plastic tubes and sent out to sea from Stavanger, which is in Norway, 'to drift where fate would take them'. But he didn't really put that drawing in the tube, did he? He could have put in a blank sheet of paper. He did. It was with the fish. He could make another drawing but it wouldn't be the same.

The owner of the café was a Turkish man in his fifties who turned up at random intervals with crates of Coke and supplies of bread and salami and jars of sun-dried tomatoes in the boot of his car. One morning he had a call from Penny, who told him she wouldn't be coming in any more. No reason given; calling him had been courtesy enough. When he asked Imogen if she knew of anyone who could step in, she suggested Robert.

For Imogen, work was a healthy thing; and art, she'd decided long ago, wasn't work. It wasn't the *only* healthy thing, Robert wanted to suggest, but he respected her choice. And despite her dreaminess, her appearance of being not quite there, when she needed to be she was a practical girl. She was resourceful. She cured the fridge of its rattle, and then she somehow got it to hum more quietly too. When they ran out of lettuce or milk and she went to the shops, she knew the places she could persuade to fiddle the invoice that she'd show to the Turkish man. If she could be bothered to, Robert thought, she could run a multinational corporation.

People drifted into that café with their laptops, their babies, their shopping, and drifted out again. Imogen taught Robert how to use the coffee machine: bashing out the used wet gounds, filling, tapping down, yanking home, placing the cups, switching on, frothing the milk on the thing like a trunk or a prick that sticks out, wiping it clean. For a day his heart was in it – he could even make the shape of a heart in the cappuccino froth, he enjoyed that – but then it was routine and his heart wandered off, looking for other places to graze. In the mornings the light coming in through the east-facing glass front of the café cast shadows like spiky undergrowth on the pale wood floor, then gradually died back. During the dead time, the periods when there were no customers, Imogen sat at one of the tables reading the magazines, sometimes raising her hand – no longer bandaged – and flexing her wrist, clenching and unclenching, moving her fingers and thumb to make, if the room had been darkened and you'd shone a torch, the shapes of rabbits or birds on the wall.

Sometimes Robert listened to Lionel talking about the book he claimed to be writing. Lionel was in his late fifties, and had perhaps never been any younger. Occasionally he walked out onto the pavement to smoke a cigarette, even when it was raining. His linen jacket was expensive but stained; his swept-back white hair was that of an actor or writer who put a lot of effort into not caring about adulation. He was a college lecturer, early retired. 'The paperwork, the admin,' he said to Robert, shaking his head, and then, in a stage whisper: 'I am dying, Egypt, dying.' Robert nodded, not understanding but complicit. Now he was researching and writing about those men who had come back from the First World War too traumatised by what they had seen to fit back easily into normal society, whatever 'normal' might mean at a time when Western culture had just killed off its own offspring, and who made their way out of the suburbs and along muddy farm tracks and into the woods and lived off the land. They built homes from old sheets of corrugated iron, they made candles from paraffin wax, they caught rabbits with snares. They were ingenious and self-reliant.

And then what? Robert asked him. What happened to these people? Lionel looked looked at Robert as if this was the most stupid question he'd ever been asked. But Robert wanted to know, he was interested, even though he could tell that Imogen wasn't. Lionel was creepy, she said. She'd once taken an espresso over to his table and seen that he wasn't using his laptop to write at all, he was watching pornography. Far from being embarrassed, he'd seemed glad that she'd noticed.

'What kind of porn?'

Japanese, she said, and Robert had no idea what she meant.

People drifted into that café with the loose ends of their lives. Either Robert or Imogen took their orders and then they listened, they couldn't not, to the bubbles of laughter, the oh-my-gods, the odd phrases that rose to the surface: 'That wasn't Genghis Khan, that was ... a central defender, maybe a left back ... he's gay as a coot, I should know ... had to be re-indexed from scratch ... so I shot him.' There was the occasional tramp they let sleep in a corner if he wasn't smelling too bad. With the druggies who wanted free food, Imogen was far more forceful than Robert in saying no and acting on it.

If someone really had been shot, they could have given the police a pretty exact description of the suspect. They were bystanders, with time on their hands to watch and take things in, and except to each other they were invisible. They were the extras on a film set who spend most of their time waiting around for the filming to start – waiting because there's a technical hitch or the lead actor is still asleep, or because the light is too bright or not bright enough or from the wrong angle. There is no right angle, they come to understand; there is only patience, and its wearing thin. And then the scenes are shot out of order: couples marrying before they have met, children growing up before they are conceived, people being buried before they die. No one has told them the whole story, but they understand that this is how it has to be, so that when they act surprised they are not just acting.

Though after waiting a whole morning and still the main actors haven't turned up, they begin thinking, let them sleep, we can do what they do.

'He's cheating on me,' Imogen drawled, 'but I'm not supposed to know.'

Did she really have a boyfriend? Robert still didn't know. But they were play-acting. They were on location, out in a field above some high cliffs, and he imagined her lounging in some state-of-the-art caravan, stripped down to her bra and skirt – it was hot as a sauna in there. Though he did wonder whether, if she knew the man was cheating and he knew that she knew, and both of them were just pretending she didn't, is that still cheating?

'I'll take him out,' he said. 'Waste him. I'll strangle the bastard.'

Imogen sighed. Without his padding and his mask, he was Batman-lite. She leant back and applied moisturiser to her neck, smoothing it in, her fingers pausing at the collarbone as if they weren't expecting it. Somewhere off to the side was another caravan in which five fat men were sitting in a circle, chewing tobacco and taking turns to spit into a small bowl on the floor. Often they missed; they were rehearsing.

'I'll rescue you,' he said.

'Do I look like a woman who wants to be rescued?'

'You deserve better than this.'

'Can you cook?' she asked him. 'Can you sew? Are you any good at spelling?'

'I can save the world,' Robert said.

'Oh, that.'

He could have hit her then, or he could have done a kind of lightning bunched-up somersault and suddenly he'd be standing on the ceiling, upside down. His head would be somewhere around her knees. His grin would be a frown. Coins would fall from his pockets. He'd take a few paces forward and back. Admittedly this would be more impressive if he was wearing his full costume and working in a less confined space, but even if they were outside and she had pushed him off the edge of the cliff, he could see that bouncing back for more would soon get annoying.

'That's not saving the world,' she said. 'That's walking upside down.'

In the evening, when the light was dying and the director sent them home, Robert imagined that as they walked back into town they'd see rooks swirling and then gathering on a single tree. This tree, the rooks would be signalling, this one. As they approached the rooks would move to another tree and then to another, moving deeper into the forest, until finally they would reach where they were meant to go. It would be dangerous and dark, but they'd be wearing little plastic fluorescent animals on the backs of their jackets and they would be safe.

∼

Then Imogen's uncle died – another one, not the one who was already dead but one Robert had known nothing about (how many were there?), who had been living in Canada and who had been very dear to her, something he had to take her word for because that morning she seemed more upset by the fact she'd never been to Canada than by anything else. But what was he to know? She was vegetarian. She'd had a phase when she thought she was gay but now she wasn't. She liked Japanese films (but not the pornographic ones, or maybe it was just Lionel). It didn't add up to much. Most people you think you know are really just surfacing for air from a whole invisible realm of other people, parents and cousins and lovers and teachers and colleagues and role models even, and who can guess who those are, and her uncle's death had sent Imogen back into that realm. Robert couldn't reach her. He wasn't a member of the clan. He told her to go home, that he could manage the café by himself for a day or so, but she said she needed the routine and the distraction of things to do.

Distraction was what she got, because that day the local madwoman paid them a visit. They could hear her marching up and down the street and shouting at random pedestrians: 'You haven't got it! You've got it! You haven't got it!' She wasn't a baglady. She was in her late twenties, smartly dressed, bright-eyed; she could have been an over-eager marketing consultant with a lapel badge who'd got lost on the way to the conference. But she was doing this thing, in people's faces.

She came to the door of the café and peered in through the glass. Then she stuck out one finger and pushed the door as if to test it was really a door and she came inside, and maybe a sour little breeze slipped in with her. Lionel wasn't there that day but there was another man, younger, with a laptop, and two women with a child in a buggy, and a table with three or four men staring at some spreadsheets. None of them looked up, none of them wanted to make eye contact. 'You haven't got it!' she shouted at the laptop guy. Robert took hold of her wrist – it was cold, like touching something inside the fridge – and she shouted 'You haven't got it!' in his face but she left, she wasn't going to make an issue of it, except that ten minutes later she was back and standing over the table with the spreadsheets – one of the men had got it, the others didn't. The way everyone was ignoring her and the laptop man began typing faster than words could be thought of struck Robert as funny, but at the same time he found himself willing the madwoman to go up to Imogen and shout 'You've got it!' Even though what *it* was, he had no idea. It could have been some disease, but he didn't think it was.

The Turkish man came through the door carrying a box of muffins. He saw the madwoman and growled. He was short and wide and gruff, and he had the weight of the Ottoman empire on his shoulders, its history and legacy, and he didn't have time for complications, he barely had time to shave. The madwoman jerked her head round and stared at him. He told her to get out. 'You've got it!' she shouted back. 'You've got it!' He said he'd call the police, and he put down the box to get his mobile out from his jacket. The woman reached inside the cardboard box and started throwing muffins at him, and then at everyone else. A glass was knocked to the floor and smashed, and the child in the buggy started crying. The Turkish man tried to grab her arm but she slipped free like water and mashed a muffin into his face – this was a woman with an *appetite*, with a serious need to rearrange things. Robert saw that Imogen had gone into dreamy mode, about-to-cry mode, and no one else seemed to take in what was really happening, not until they heard the police-car siren at the end of the street, which made it official.

It was what Imogen needed, that day. It was hardly even what's called an *incident* – for all the padded high-tech accessories bulking out their youth, the couple of policemen were just going to drive the madwoman into the next borough and drop her off and leave it to the next lot to think up a better idea – but after the Turkish man had left Imogen sat on the floor, tears streaming down her face, brushing muffin crumbs off her shoulder. 'It's too late,' she said, and when Robert asked what for she said she'd probably never go to Canada now, or Samarkand or Mongolia or even New York, and this wasn't a job, it was just playing at being someone with a job, and for wasting four years of her life making coffee for the chit-chattering rich – babies, books, *spreadsheets*: if you pricked them they would not bleed at all – she deserved worse than RSI and she'd forgotten to tell the Turkish man they needed more mushrooms. Robert told her no, it wasn't too late. She looked at him as if to ask if this was just something someone said. They left the rest of the clearing up for the next day. They closed early.

∽

In 1870, when Paris was surrounded by the army of Prussia

and the besieged citizens were reduced to eating dogs and rats and the animals from the zoo – not sparing even the elephants, Castor and Pollux – Manet's letters to his wife were among those sent out of the city by balloon. They used pigeons too: the letters were rolled up and inserted into goose quills attached to their tail feathers. Neither method came with a guarantee: both balloons and pigeons could be blown off course or shot down by hunters or army snipers. On 5 October Manet wrote: 'We can't really say what's happening here since letters that leave by balloon could fall into enemy hands ...'

This was what had happened to the job applications that Robert had written – occasionally he'd had a short and merciless reply but most had drifted 'where fate would take them', as his artist friend had said, or had been intercepted by the enemy. He'd given up. But for Imogen, it was worth trying again. He went to the post office and bought a hundred first-class stamps and together they wrote a hundred letters to captains of industry, big people at big companies, telling them what a valuable contribution Imogen could make to their business. They used words like *teamwork*, *initiative*, and because she'd been to art college they felt it was OK to use *creative*; they drew the line at *dynamic*, there were limits. Lionel insisted on giving her a reference on headed paper filched from the college he'd taught at: he'd known Imogen intimately for many years, he wrote, and she was an honest and hardworking girl. Then they made coffee and sat back and waited.

This was painting-by-numbers, but they knew it was also moving-on time: the madwoman had served them notice. Imogen became light-hearted, as if she had already left. She had her hair cut professionally and looked like a model; she bought a pale green blouse patterned with what

Robert said looked like commas or raindrops or tears. 'Or sperm?' she said. 'Wriggling their way?' *Today's special,* she wrote in chalk on the menu board: *Côtelettes de chien aux petits pois.* They were liberal with the chilli sauce and they put up the prices of the toasted paninis and very few people even noticed.

Once in a while – luck, fate, the hand of God – a pigeon gets through. A reply came in from a law company with offices in the middle of town, and Imogen went to see them and she started the next Monday.

Robert stayed on. Bereft and elated, abandoned but suddenly possessed of his own kingdom, for a couple of days he managed the café on his own. Then Penny came back, her hair still yanked back in the same rubber band, he could have sworn it, and he found it hard to like her. She was noisier than Imogen and less in two worlds but also less practical and she had no idea how to stop the fridge from rattling. Although she'd been away she still considered herself Robert's senior. She made him feel lost, as if he had to begin all over again.

The machine that toasted the paninis set fire to itself and the Turkish man brought in a replacement, a second-hand one, which also broke down, and meanwhile Lionel tip-tapped away at his corner table, and one day a woman came in and sat down opposite him and watched him typing for forty minutes in silence. Lionel barely glanced up. Then the woman asked for a glass of tap water, drank it in one long gulp, and left. But she was back the next day, and this time Robert recognised her. She was in disguise, with day-glo pink highlights in her hair and wearing jeans, no longer the trainee marketing consultant, or perhaps that had been the disguise. Caged in, medicated, she was the madwoman, the muffin-thrower.

The woman was young enough to be Lionel's daughter. She *was* his daughter, Penny said. Or one of his students from the college where he had taught, stalking him, seeking revenge for low grades. After ten minutes of silence and a glass of tap water the woman began talking to Lionel, and he talked back, and though they were speaking in whispers their words were heard by everyone in the café. She wasn't his daughter. She was snuffling, she had a cold, and she told him that she'd woken at 5 a.m. with no covering because he had hogged the whole duvet, and she'd watched the dawn and it was grim. She *always* had a cold, he said, she was never not sick. Which might have something to do with him, she suggested, hogging the whole duvet every fucking night? As if she wasn't in his life at all, as if she didn't exist?

She turned to Robert on her way out but he felt she was looking right through him, that it was he who didn't exist.

Penny told Robert she'd had an email from Imogen. Within weeks she had become the boss's right hand. It was all about the *culture*, apparently. Everyone in law comes into it from law school, and the way things get done and people behave is governed by the textbooks, precedents and torts and all the Latin words. Then someone walks in off the street and says hold on, think about it, what are you fussing with that for, why don't you try doing it this way? Imogen was that person.

Lionel would come into the café at around eleven o'clock and open up his laptop and order an espresso, and half an hour or an hour later, or sometimes not until the afternoon, the woman would come in and sit opposite him and after a while the whispering would start again: his lack of ambition, the idiocy of ambition, the necessity and hopelessness of ambition; the failure to recognise what the other needed, the failure to recognise what *oneself* needed or even wanted; infinite omissions and derelictions and comings-up-short. On a day when they were they were pushing hard on the domestic detail, down where the snakes were slithering – the rubbish bags, the laundry, who never washes the pans, who *burns* the pans, who never buys loo roll, whose hair is matting the shower drain – Penny looked at Robert and grinned and turned to the table where Lionel and the woman were whispering and made a shape with her hands, the shape, Robert caught on, of a camera. Maybe Penny wasn't so unpractical after all. This was theatre, it was art, they could charge an entrance fee and get written up in *Time Out*.

He was infantile, the woman told Lionel, he'd missed out on potty-training and hadn't got it in him to grow up, and no wonder, given the emotionally stunted dwarves that had spawned him. She was the most selfish person he'd ever met, Lionel replied from behind his laptop, she just took and took and the reason she never gave was because she had nothing in her to give, he could tap any part of her and it would ring hollow. She told him his prick tasted of rotten horse-meat, it was dogfood. He said her breasts were so flat they were below sea-level, he said her cunt smelled of Swedish herring.

Around them, anywhere within the four walls, people couldn't help but listen. They pretended to read books, pretended to make lesson plans, pretended to drink coffee, pretended not to see the madwoman's black eye and the bruise on her jaw.

Lionel folded down his laptop, scraped back his chair and stood up and walked out of the door. The woman's hair was strung out, her cheeks were wet with tears. Penny went over with a glass of water and rested her hand on the woman's shoulder and Robert saw that she, the woman, was crazed – to put herself in line for so much hurt was madness, error – but this wasn't theatre and she wasn't playing. Saw, with only a glimmer of understanding, the glimmer that filters through the leaves of the trees as you trudge up the muddy path to your tumbledown shelter, animals coupling in the bracken. Voles, or rabbits. Look away and they've gone – nature's indifference – but they'll be back, or others. The woman was both furious with Lionel and feeding off him, she was ravenous. She'd have gone to the guillotine. She was *ancien régime*, and doomed.

Another email from Imogen to Penny. Her boss was single, rich, not old, not ugly. She was flying off with him to a conference in New York. 'Reader, she married him,' Robert said, and Penny laughed. Imogen was a modern girl, she wasn't the marrying kind. He stepped out of the café and saw Lionel standing further up the pavement, laptop clamped tight under his elbow as he tried to light a cigarette in the wind.

FLIPPERTIGIBBET

After our father left, our mother would often pause while doing the washing-up and stare out of the kitchen window over the sink, would pause for so long that the water would go cold. She was looking not, I think, at the potting shed, the wooden hut at the back of the garden where my father used to spend so many hours alone, but at the sparrows and starlings bobbing around the bird-feeder that hung from the tree in front of it. It's always movement that attracts the eye.

My sister has no memory of this. Nor does she remember the woman who disappeared. This was in the 1950s – a long time ago, my sister reminds me, as if a line has been drawn. We lived in Yorkshire in what was more of a dormitory suburb than a village, within easy commuting distance of Leeds, so during the day most of the men disappeared too, but we knew roughly where they had gone to and usually they came home at night, even if I didn't see them then because I was in bed. The woman who disappeared lived in the row of terraced houses at the top of the field where we went sledging in winter, and if her name – which was Mrs Bishop: a man's name, not a woman's – and the fact of her disappearance are all I can tell my sister – not who she was or what she did or whether she was ever found – this is because no one else seemed to know or even to care very much either, although there must have been some gossip in the pub and at the hairdresser's. I don't even know if she was married, though I assume not, because if she was there'd have been a Mr Bishop left over, and I remember no such person.

For the grown-ups the war was still very close, almost yesterday, and the war was a time when people were always going missing. My father never spoke of it, nor did we ask him to, though at some point I did learn that he had been in the D-Day landings. For my older sister and me the war was unknown, hidden, locked in a cupboard, but I'm sure it was still present in our lives in many and contradictory ways. The war was behind the rising birth rate, in the hurry to get on with repopulating the world. It was behind both my mother's fondness for bright colours and eagerness for fun and my father's caution and strictness, and it may have been behind his letting go of those things too. It was a legend that explained things even when it didn't. Some years later, when I was in my early teens and at a new school, a boy who had somehow got wind of the fact that my father was no longer around asked me if he had been killed in the war. Chronologically, biologically, this was an impossibility. But I said yes – I was going downstairs at the time, a steep set of steps into a basement room where there were two table-tennis tables, and I couldn't stop myself – and my father thereby became heroic and some of his heroism rubbed off on me, which was something I needed, and for a time I was believed.

My sister would have been angry if she'd known I had said this. She was always, even then, the bookish one in the family, by which I mean the stickler for accuracy. Nowadays she seems to me a disappointed woman. Money, profit, she says, everything is driven by the markets. Standards are slipping. No one pays attention any more; no one is *paid* to pay attention. Even though it's she who cannot recall my mother looking out of the kitchen window, or even the sparrows. It's my sister who disappeared, I sometimes think, and the person who replaced her I don't know.

Recently I watched – in a hotel room in New York, as it happens, a place my mother surely dreamt of, with its air conditioning and its plumped-up pillows and its curtains you opened by pulling a cord – the film of a novel written by Raymond Chandler in the 1940s, and then a discussion about it afterwards. A film in black and white: that, to her, given my choice of so many channels, would have been a puzzle. Chandler went to Hollywood to write the screenplay too – for money, why else. And then, when the director took over the scriptwriting, he noticed a small difficulty: a loose end, a spare and unexplained body. He called up Chandler and asked who did kill this character. Search me, said Chandler. Loose ends, oversights, mistakes – these days people go looking for them, shining bright torches, so there seem to be more of them, but it doesn't mean they haven't always happened. It doesn't mean either that they can always be explained, or even that, in the end, they really matter, or change the outcome. The little ones, that is, though who can tell at the time.

My mother knew this, instinctively. My mother, if she'd heard me tell that boy on the basement stairs that my father had been killed in the war, would have laughed. Mistakes, for her, even deliberate ones, were no cause for moral outrage. If I'd lied then I'd be found out, and that was punishment enough. If I'd meant it as a joke, well, there were better ones, but jokes in principle were good. My mother laughed often. She liked pretty clothes and new perfumes and the kind of music you could dance to. One of my earliest memories is of sitting on her knee at the bedroom dressing table, playing with her little coloured bottles and the hinged sides of the three-way mirror. She liked magazines with photographs of film stars, and because my father was tight with money she got the hairdresser to pass on the old ones – which put my father in a bind: the magazines he thought childish, but he had to approve of the thrift. She was quick and light and small, and if you'd have said petite she'd have laughed for both shame and enjoyment, and because the word is French. Are sparrows petite? She was, she said, a flippertigibbet. She said this at first mischievously, delighting in what was perceived by both herself and others as her irresponsibility; and then, after our father left, regretfully and self-accusingly, as if it was her love of bright colours that had driven him away.

She was wrong, both before and after. There are bright colours and dull ones, and a preference for the former doesn't make a person more flighty than someone who prefers the latter. I'd go further: I'd say that my mother was right to prefer pinks and yellows and blues to browns and greys. But of course I would say this. I, to my mother's extreme delight and continual puzzlement – the boy, not the girl – work as a fashion journalist, and go on trips abroad such as the one to New York when I chanced to see the Chandler film and vaguely wondered if she'd seen it herself. And as for our father leaving, this may well have been because she wasn't flippertigibbet *enough*.

My father did, much later, settle for a brown-and-grey woman, but at the time he left home he was having an affair with a woman who made my mother, in comparison, appear a paragon of conformity and good taste.

Lisa was part French, which seemed to serve as some

explanation as to the way things were. She spoke with an accent that made her interesting. She wasn't married; or at least, there was no husband in evidence. Her two sons had been fathered by different men; this was not something anyone bothered to tell us, my sister and me, but at some point we just knew, and our parents knew we knew. She lived above the village on what I can't call a farm but might call a smallholding, if that's the word for a bungalow down a track with a field or two attached and a scatter of hens and cats. She dressed for outdoors, in a thick man's overcoat and layers of scarves. She looked older than our mother but I doubt she was. The bungalow was cold, as much a garage as a home, with boxes and seats ripped from old cars for chairs and bits of machinery and barbed wire lying around. The one time we were in that building my mother chose not to sit down.

Why were we there anyway? A good reason would have been delivering Lisa's sons, the older of whom was called Alan, back home, but I can't recall a single occasion when Alan and his brother came over to play at our house. They killed rabbits, we understood. They threw stones. Their attendance at school was erratic. The younger brother, the one who was not called Alan, was oddly quiet and then got into furious tempers; he was probably, we'd say now, autistic. I think my mother was simply curious, and took me and my sister along for cover.

That our father at some point began sharing Lisa's bed – Lisa's *damp* bed, with the sheets unwashed for weeks – was beyond guessing. Though when the time eventually came for my parents to sit my sister and me down at the kitchen table – a family occasion, obscurely like Christmas – and tell us that our father was leaving, and an 'other woman' was mentioned and Lisa's name was spoken, I don't think

I gasped in disbelief. Our father, after all, had been in the war and had fought in France. He too liked tinkering with things, in his case plants and bulbs and seeds, which he did in the the potting shed at the bottom of our garden. Besides, the adult world had its own laws, impenetrable to me; I didn't expect to understand them.

If there had to be an other woman, there was an obvious candidate, if only because our family and hers were already entwined. But this would have been comic, even farcical. Our father was a short man, and walked in a hunched manner as if against an opposing wind. Mrs Morris, the daughter of an army colonel, was the tallest woman we knew. She had, we believed, whiskers, and she had six children, and she had set about this with military precision. If she had been allowed, I'm sure she would have made an even more efficient colonel than her father: killed more of the enemy, finished off the war in half the time. Even now, whenever I come across a road bordered by trees planted at regular intervals – France has plenty of these – I think of Mrs Morris and her six children born at intervals of two years, a man-made landscape as opposed to a natural one in which children appear in clusters, or with irregular gaps between them. David, Liz, Andrew, Jeremy, Ann, Michael. On the age chart, my sister and I slotted in somewhere between Andrew and Ann. We mingled with them every day, both at school and in our homes, to the point where we were almost honorary members of the Morris family. But if there was no relationship between our father and Mrs Morris – and I'm certain there wasn't – beyond nods and greetings when they happened to meet, beyond small talk over sherry at Christmas and words of advice about investments or second-hand cars, between our mother and Mrs Morris there was something going on that was more than politeness. Our mother laughed at Mrs Morris, both to her face and behind her back – her rank, her correctness, her bounty – while also being in awe of her. Mrs Morris had made a go of things. Our mother had done her bit – my sister and I were the evidence – but that was as far as she could or would go in that direction, and in the other direction of the magazines, the dance music, she was stymied. Our father never brought in much income; she was accustomed to measuring things out. She wasn't, at least in the way I have called my sister, a disappointed woman; she made do, without complaint. But there was also a restlessness in her, a tingling, and it was this to which Mrs Morris responded. Being a colonel's daughter has its advantages but I guess the responsibilities can be tiring, and tiresome. Mrs Morris was amused and baffled by my mother and I think sincerely fond of her. She adopted my mother as a kind of regimental mascot.

There was, before I recall the particular day on which my mother proved once and for ever that she was not a flippertigibbet, this additional and to a child wonderful fact about Mrs Morris: her solution to the problem of conveying a large family – plus two dogs, I had forgotten the dogs – from A to B had been to purchase a second-hand hearse and convert the rear into a children's room, with benches. A panel with a sliding window separated this part from Mrs Morris and whoever happened to be seated beside her in the front. Any journey undertaken in this vehicle, even if only to church or the crescent of shops just off the main road, took the form of a royal pageant. People stopped on the pavement and waved.

And now here we are, long ago, my sister and I and the Morris children and maybe half a dozen others in the back of the hearse, off for a picnic on the moors at Ilkley on a summer afternoon. This is perhaps a year before our father left home, when he was still pottering in the potting shed, but our mother is here with us, in the passenger seat in front. The dogs, a Labrador and a smaller brown one, a terrier of some kind, are clambering over our legs and sniffing at the picnic hampers, inside one of which there is a cake which mustn't be squashed – for which of the Morris children it hardly matters, they all have birthdays in June or July. The sky is blue, the sun warm. I am wearing my favourite Aertex check shirt. The only surprise is that among the extra children today are Alan and his brother, Lisa's boys. Mrs Morris is determined to show that her command is infinite, encompassing not just the food and the weather but potential spoilsports too.

There are rocks at Ilkley to climb, thick bracken to hide in, steep paths along which to stage ambushes. Casualties are minor: a grazed knee, a spot of dizziness from too much sun, a child or a dog being sick. Nothing the colonel's daughter cannot cope with. But then something odd: Alan's younger brother begins to hiccup, and it seems he cannot stop, and he spits at whoever comes near him. For the other children, my sister and I included, this is funny – under a certain age, there's something indecently exciting about drool and saliva. My mother too takes this lightly: just keep out of range, she tells us. But Mrs Morris is more concerned; she knows that the longer this goes on, the worse it's going to get. So we leave earlier than planned. We bag up the litter, we fold the rugs, and we are back in the hearse, driving back not, Mrs Morris has decided, along the main road down in the valley, but along the top road across the moors, which will bring us more directly to the home of Alan and his brother, and it is here that the trouble begins.

A mile or so before the village, the traffic on the narrow

road is at a standstill. In the back, sweaty and packed tightly together and stuffed with cake, it takes us some time to realise that we are not moving, but when we do Alan and his brother seize their chance. They manage to open the back of the hearse and escape, climbing over a wall and setting off across a field towards their home, the bungalow. The dogs are quickly after them and then, for no good reason other than that this is a birthday party and here is another game to be played, the other children are climbing out of the back of the hearse too and are climbing over the wall and chasing Alan and his brother.

My sister and I stand in the road, torn between joining the chase and loyalty to our mother. Neither of us has that gang mentality that can come from being a member of a large family, from being too many to be constantly observed. From somewhere in front of us, beyond the cars lined up in the road, the siren of an ambulance or police car can be heard. Mrs Morris, whose own children are among the mutineers, grips the steering wheel tightly. My sister and I look towards her, expecting her to start shouting orders, to re-assert her authority, but she seems frozen in uncertainty, though now I think that she is making rapid calculations. One of these concerns the queue of traffic at a standstill: it's more than possible that at the next cross-roads, a notorious local black spot, there has been an accident, and surely it is preferable for the children to run across the field, from where they can drop down through a small wood to the village, than for them to pass by at walking speed the mangled wreck of a car and its occupants.

It's my mother who takes command. We see her lips move: she is counting and naming the children who are running in the field. Then she looks back into the rear of the hearse. *Where's Mussie?* she asks.

Mussie is a five-year-old girl, one of the extra children from the village who have joined the outing. Questioned, neither I nor my sister can recall seeing Mussie in the hearse on the way back. We have left Mussie behind.

Someone has to drive back to Ilkley; someone has to stay and take charge of the scattering children. Mrs Morris – how *could* she have not taken a roll call? – surrenders the hearse unconditionally. She gets out of the driving seat, clambers over the wall, and with long, loping strides follows in the wake of the children. And I wonder now – though I am still as ignorant about this as I was then as a child – if another calculation has not been made. Suppose my father's affair with Lisa had already begun at this time; in which case a Saturday afternoon with everyone away on a picnic might have been an opportunity too good to miss. Suppose too that Mrs Morris, who made it her business to know everything that was going on in the village, who knew the point of gossip but never gossiped herself, was informed of the affair. Given this, Mrs Morris, who I'm sure viewed my mother as a kind of child, with all the innocence that word invokes, would have wanted to protect her.

Any such reasoning is of no concern to my mother. She has first, of course, to adjust the driving seat so that her feet can reach the pedals. Then she has to find the right gears, and push and pull and somehow turn around that unwieldy hearse in the narrow road, among the press of other cars. She has never previously driven anything larger than a baby Austin.

With my sister and I sitting with her in the front, my mother drove back to Ilkley. We found Mussie in the care of the owner of an ice-cream van, with raspberry sauce all over her face.

We took the top road again on the way back, but now there was no queue of traffic; any accident had been cleared away. Nor on that late Saturday afternoon do I remember any witnesses to my mother's triumph on the long, steep lane that led down into the village, but triumph it was. Not only had she had got to grips with that ridiculous vehicle and broken it in, but a child had disappeared and my mother had brought her back. At the top of the hill she switched off the engine: petrol rationing was still in force – my sister will correct me on this if I'm wrong – a hangover from the war, and this was a ruse my father had taught her. Thrift, thrift, but pleasure too from the silent free-wheeling downhill glide.

DISTRACTION

Rick phoned. He was back. He wanted to meet me and suggested the Slow Man.

He shook his head, wonderingly, when I asked him how was it, and I took this to mean not good. He looked as if he'd been smuggled home in the back of a lorry. Where had he been? I'd forgotten.

'Portugal.'

'Of course.'

'Portugal is not the point.'

He sighed. He ran his hand through his hair and I felt like a schoolboy who's trying hard but will never get it. 'Have you brought it with you?'

There was a pause then, while a girl who sometimes worked in the bar brushed by, a girl with her hair cut high and short at the back, and I'd still never laid a finger on her neck, but what he meant, it turned out, was £3,000 in cash, and I hadn't a clue what he was talking about.

He took me through it. He had a girlfriend, Tina. I'd met her: slim, bright, with big wide eyes that didn't blink. A week before he'd gone with Tina to Portugal he'd sold his car to a cash buyer. He didn't want to put the money in the bank because his account was joint, with his wife. He didn't want to open a new account because he knew he'd just spend that money while he was away. He wanted it intact, a cushion for a safe landing in case Portugal turned out to be not exactly a honeymoon, and so he'd given it to me to look after, a safe pair of hands. All of this made sense, except for the last bit.

He'd been away for longer than he'd expected, for three months, but still.

I worked at that time as a press officer for a national charity so I was, in Rick's eyes, a good person. I supported the underdogs. I didn't forget things, and though I'd made a few mistakes none of them were mortal sins, nothing that couldn't be shrugged off with a few beers. I was a safe bet, and he'd lost, and neither of us could explain this.

How thick is a wad of notes that add up to £3,000 – an inch? Two? You couldn't just lose that money down a crack in the floorboards. And for me not to even remember it, how big was the hole in my head? Though I did, sometime into our third pint, recall the ghost of a brown envelope, and something turned over in the pit of my stomach leaving a hollow the shape of that same grubby envelope. Maybe I'd donated it to the charity. Maybe I'd climbed to a high place and scattered the notes to the wind.

We went to my flat and we searched, turned everything upside down. Really it should have been Rick looking while I stood back, because if I'd hidden it I'd know where it was – when the police do a raid, they don't leave searching to the dealers. But Rick was so frantic he kept missing places, so while he was emptying drawers it was me doing the detailed work – in the lining of my jackets, under the cutlery tray. Inside a bicycle pump – *there* would be a good place to hide the money, if I ever had to go through this again. Except whenever you have a puncture, you can never find the pump. Nothing.

Rick stayed over. He had nowhere else to go. The girl,

Tina, hadn't come back with him, was still in Portugal, and his wife had changed the locks. So for a few weeks we wound around each other, two dogs in the same cage, me owing him money but him with a rent-free space, both of us waiting for it to break.

One night he came home from the Slow Man drunk, and hit me. He had to do this, to get it over with, and I was glad he was drunk when it happened because his blows were less sharp than they should have been, he was going through the motions. But I did hit back. Otherwise we'd have had to do this thing again and again. I caught him on the forehead and broke my finger. It sobered him up, and on me it had the opposite effect. This was in the kitchen, a place with so many knives and sharp edges it's a wonder we didn't kill each other, and at one point when we were on the floor, kicking against the baseboards, trying to both stay out of the reach of hurt and get closer, which came to the same thing, I started to feel happy, enjoyment, relief, because I knew this wasn't about the money at all, it was about the girl he'd left behind in Portugal, and there was nothing I could do about that, nothing I could be held responsible for. Though I wasn't going to win, I knew that too. I was going to lose, or we both were. He smashed my jaw and I bit my tongue and felt my teeth shift and com-plain in their sockets, and once we'd both tasted blood we could stop.

I went into the bathroom to clean up. I tried not to look too long in the mirror. The light was too bright: you don't need 100 watts to see your own face. The cap on the tooth-paste tube, I noticed, wasn't the same as it used to be, it was somehow chunkier. And now that it was in my hand, I saw that my toothbrush was designed like a miniature high-speed train. The world was changing around me so fast I couldn't keep track. I could focus on only one thing at a time. Everything else slipped under the radar.

∾

Rick had once told me how the toothpaste companies could increase their profits overnight by enlarging the exit hole just slightly, a millimetre, a millimetre and a half if they were greedy, so that people would get to the end of the tube quicker. He was going to take this idea to Colgate in a sealed envelope, persuade them of its value, and get them to promise him 10 per cent before opening it. Why would they do that? If he wanted to, he could persuade people.

One person he'd recently been trying to persuade, though not about toothpaste, was the girl at the Slow Man with the long neck. After Rick left I made a move of my own, only to find that she belonged in every possible way to the old West Indian man after whom the bar was named, who took for ever to serve a drink. He was a role model of sorts, and now even more so. Neither Rick nor I stood a chance. We were both being punished. I found this reassuring, as though it made us equals.

The fight we'd had was the kind that can make blood-brothers out of casual friends, but in our case it didn't. Portugal had come between Rick and me, not just the broken trust but the slow sad songs he'd picked up in the bars of Lisbon, and we grew apart. But Rick did OK, did more than OK. He found a new girl, this one from a rich family, and after he got her pregnant her father lent them money to buy a flat, and he was up and running. This was the 90s. Buy a flat, add in a jacuzzi and sell it on for double. Buy two more flats. Do nothing even, just stay in bed for a month blowing bubbles, and he was still richer when he put his clothes back on and stepped outside. Each of us is born with a password; most us never find the place it unlocks but Rick, Rick had found the door. He bought a house in the suburbs for his ex-wife and children. In the summer I'd see him cruising around in an open-top Mercedes. He had reached a certain level of immunity. When he crashed that Mercedes into a bus queue and broke a man's leg, he pleaded that he could hardly be expected to keep his eyes on the road at a time of year when there were girls in short skirts buying oranges at the market, and he was let off with a small fine.

In the late 90s a journalist with an interest in digging up dirt happened to look at the charity that employed me and added up some figures and found income unaccounted for – a figure with a whole row of noughts, besides which Rick's £3,000 was just pocket money. One of the directors had been siphoning it off for years. For *years* – you'd think someone must have known, you'd think a lot of people must have known, or maybe they didn't, maybe they just happened to be facing in the other direction. After a certain time, whatever is happening becomes the norm, the routine. But this didn't sound very convincing when it was the charity's own press officer saying it. I was out of a job.

I was unattached, as they say, and I wasn't as wedded to good works as Rick had assumed I was. Nor, obviously, was I much good at them. Who exactly had I made life better for? Not even myself. I decided to go and look for that self, even if I didn't have much expectation of finding anything; I decided to go travelling. I gave notice on my flat. While packing, I picked up some some ancient shoes at the bottom of a cupboard and they felt heavier than they should have, and I knew what was in there even before my fingers touched it.

I phoned Rick's office and made an appointment.

'Count it,' I told him.

It was summer, a hot day, and to get to his office I'd walked through the park. I remember that day. I was feeling good, I was making a clean break. I was coming out of a long tunnel, or a corridor with names on all the doors made up of those letters you can move around or replace but whatever they spell the rooms behind those doors are still prison cells, and I was a free man. I remember stopping in front of a tree and not even closing my eyes but just listening to all the sounds we usually filter out: traffic noise, the occasional siren, children's voices, birdsong. I wasn't in a hurry.

I told the girl on reception that he was expecting me.

'Count it.'

He glanced at the envelope I'd placed on his desk and nodded. Then he opened a drawer and swept the money into it. On the wall behind him was a photograph of a woman and child, I assumed his new family. His hair was sleeked down and he had put on weight. He didn't need that money now, I needed it a lot more than he did and he knew this and he could have told me to keep it but we both knew that's not how the world works. He didn't want to give me the pleasure of refusing it.

After so long, I still felt the bruise on my jaw. If he wasn't even going to bother to count the money then I could at least make him answer a simple question.

'Do you ever hear from Tina?' I asked him. 'Where is she now?'

He closed the drawer and looked away, looked through the window at the blue sky with not a cloud in it. He still loved her, he said. He loved her to distraction, except he pronounced it wrong.

43

I thought he was drunk. 'Distraction,' I said.

'Distración,' he repeated. She'd left Portugal a long time ago and this was where she now was: a place in South America, a small town in the middle of nowhere, a town where the wind blew dust through the streets and most of the men had left for the city and the old people's dreams were troubled by jackals. He laughed. It wasn't a laugh I warmed too, it was harsh as the wind blowing through those streets, but I had a feeling he was telling the truth.

BACK ROW, FOURTH FROM THE RIGHT

The sun was doing its best but clouds kept blowing over. Have you noticed, when it's both windy and sunny, people tend to laugh more? Or can't make up their minds. It could be one thing or the other. Out on the lawn in front of the hotel Geoffrey chivvied us to our places while the photographer tried to look not just at Bella.

Geoff could be needlessly aggressive, in the way of many men who are short, but he also had charm. Once he'd lined us up on either side of two chairs, the taller ones at the back, he and Bella sat down on the chairs and the photographer clicked. More than once, maybe half a dozen times in all, so that Geoff could choose the shot that did us least bad justice, or the one that was most flattering of Bella. You never get everyone not frowning or picking their nose at exactly the same time.

This was all a long time ago, not pre-history but when there was still such a thing as history, before it all collapsed online, everything jostling together in a kind of watery soup – everything from the causes of the First World War to naked Bella lookalikes spreading their legs at the click of a keyboard button, so that no one has to put their memory or imagination to the test or even stand up from their chair.

The photograph itself is a museum piece. If I ever had a copy of it myself it disappeared many moons ago, and the one I'm looking at now is borrowed from Tom (back row, far left), whose habits as well as his dress code remain unchanged since the time they were forged, perhaps even since they were genetically programmed in the womb. He keeps things. He files them in logical places. He'd been trained as a historian (*'an* historian', we used to say), or at least had a history degree. He had a radio in his office tuned to the classical music programme and in summer to the cricket; in the previous generation he'd have smoked a pipe.

Geoffrey was our tribal chieftain. He drove a shiny red sports car and when he went abroad he flew first class and Bella, who was just right for the passenger seat of that car and whom he'd acquired on one of those foreign trips, was his new wife – in her twenties, maybe half Geoff's age, slim and lively and kittenish and with a blue flashing light over her tumbling blonde curls as a warning to any of us who were tempted to stray beyond our job descriptions. But Geoffrey hadn't risen up the ladder by accident. He paid us well enough to keep our frustrations damped down – it's a fine line: if you pay too little the serfs rebel, if you pay too much they think the rules don't apply to them – and on the whole we played safe. We knew our places. Me, I'm right behind the seated couple, just to the left, next to Joyce as it happens, who is looking a bit sulky, bored with the whole procedure. I remember Joyce. I have no reason to believe that Joyce remembers me. Ben is front row, third from the left. Or he is back row, fourth from the right. That was Ben all over: he wasn't interested in declaring his presence, he could slot in easily in either row.

That I recall this photograph being taken is because,

except for this one time, it didn't happen. There was a work ethic and there was a play ethic, and neither involved standing in a row in the sunshine and wind and being told to grin. What we did, as a group, was make wallpaper. Not the thing that's applied directly onto walls but the thing used to hide the walls, on shelves – books, more specifically *informational* books, packed with facts and statistics and diagrams and photographs and merry little anecdotes. Books whose contents were arranged in alphabetical order, and if they weren't they had *indexes*. Books people went to for self-improvement, even if they never actually read them. Just having them around was usually enough; they signalled a fine intention. In historical times, a profitable number of people desired such objects, and the ones that didn't go on shelves were placed on coffee tables.

None of us knew at the time that the coffee table was set to be a far longer-lived cultural institution than the kind of books we were making, but it wouldn't have bothered us. We had salaries, not pretensions. And the reason Geoff had taken us all deep into the countryside for a two-day party – it would go on the accounts as a sales conference – was to celebrate his new coup, a contract for a whole new series of books: legends of the ancient world, the history of flying machines or underwater mammals, the subject matter was irrelevant because the prose was uniform for all, polished and buffed for a state funeral. And to show off Bella, of course. She was worth the showing.

It went well, by which I mean a good part of the advance on the contract for the new books was spent on the bar tab. Some of us had arrived with partners or spouses, which offset the over-familiarity bred by spending our working days in our own exclusive company. We were there to have fun, and complaints on the first night from the hotel's other guests gave us a reputation to live up to. It went well, that is, until checking-out time on the final morning, when a fury broke loose: Bella in the lobby angry and tearful, Bella shrieking at the poor boy behind the reception desk. She was demanding not just the manager but his head on a plate. Something had been stolen from her room. Geoff was with her, trying to negotiate, but he was out of his depth. He'd wanted attention to be paid to her, but not like this. The rest of us were milling around by the entrance, hungover, with our bags packed, waiting to leave. Tom came out of the breakfast room, annoyingly hearty, and we stood by the lift and watched the show. Bella wasn't a kitten at all. She was a rabid cat, she was untouchable.

And then, some days later, into the next week, Ben came into my office, and though enough time had passed for sleep and recovery and knuckling back down to routine, it's possible I didn't even notice he'd come in until he sat down and placed an envelope on my desk. Ben moved quietly. He was young, barely into his twenties, friendly and helpful but not a joiner-in, not among the group who hung around the water cooler (did we even have a water cooler?). He dressed for winter throughout the year, in black jumpers and heavy shoes with complicated laces. He was a researcher, diligent and reliable, a team player if I wanted to be cruel. Neutral, background, asexual. But the envelope wasn't: inside that envelope was a woman's necklace, a necklace with diamonds, and I knew at once whose it was.

Jesus, Ben.

Why was he showing me this? Because he trusted me. I told him that pretty well everyone who was close to me at the time, they may have tolerated or even believed they liked me, but trusting was a different thing. So why?

Because he admired the way I *wrote*, he said. But it was hackwork, what we did, it was stringing beans, and even with the real stuff you trust the tale not the teller, he knew that. Ben said he did, and it was because I could string beans and not pretend they were pearls that he trusted me. It was meant as a compliment. He needed my help. He asked if he could stay with me for a night or two. He was in some kind of trouble, he said, and it wasn't good for him to be alone.

He came home with me that night and I put him up on the sofa with a sleeping bag and some blankets.

Back at the hotel, he'd been in Bella's room for the only reason there was to be in that room, given that Bella was there too. While the rest of us, Geoff included, had been drinking downstairs in the bar, which never closed. He'd been going to his bed and noticed, while passing another room, that the door was open and there she was, in *her* bed. He went in. She was, he said, a lovely person. I didn't doubt it. I looked at him in wonder: so skinny, so almost not there at all, and yet out of all of us it was Ben who'd pushed out, made a move, who'd penetrated the sacred grove. The whole thing was a joke with a punchline that catches you unawares, and I couldn't help but laugh. I don't mean to make light of this. I hope now, as I hoped then, that he'd had the pleasure he was entitled to. As for why, on his way out of that hotel room, he had taken her necklace, all he could say was that it had been impulsive, a sudden urge that overtook him. Could I understand that? I think I nodded. I guessed that Bella could understand it too.

But now things had changed. He hadn't seen Bella since, and had no way of contacting her, and he was being followed. He didn't know who by but he couldn't could go anywhere without this person tagging along, watching him, and he was, frankly, scared.

Ben stayed more than a night or two. He stayed several weeks. I got to know him and to like him. He did his job conscientiously because he counted himself lucky to have it, and saw it as a *way in*. I didn't disabuse him. He had a way of pausing after being asked a question as if he was writing down the answer before he spoke it, to see how it looked on paper, and yet sometimes – when I mentioned Joyce, for example, or another of the people we worked with – he shot back immediately with something deeply cutting and funny. On the side – that is, while the rest of us were variously meddling with one another's lives – he wrote stories. He showed me some, and I struggled to respond. I think I'd been bean-stringing for so long I'd forgotten how to read anything not written for money. An overall impression from memory is that many featured journeys, solitary ones; there was a desert, there were snakes, and the stories tended to just stop rather than end, leaving the reader expecting something more. This was good, I told him. Like birds flapping their wings and taking off, for reasons indecipherable by humans. He looked at me as if he was regretting having placed his life in my hands. I sometimes regretted that too. If I had been him, I'd have gone to Tom.

Meanwhile, although it's not, as a rule, a good career move to sleep with your boss's wife, especially if she's a new one, maybe Ben and maybe Bella too had known in their bones they had little to lose. The week we were due to start work on the new books, with extra staff taken on and all the desks shifted around to make room, the publisher who'd given us the contract pulled the plug. The focus groups had been disastrous, Geoff said. He waited for a response, for someone to reassure him that the books would be magnificent, but no one said anything. I doubt many of us knew then what focus groups were, but we understood that a new law had been passed: it wasn't enough to have a sure-fire idea and get to work, you now had to ask people if they liked your idea and if they didn't it was a bad one. Geoff went running around for other work and came back empty-handed. The company was winding down; we were soon to be on the streets; just beyond the horizon the internet was massing. Our bean-stringing days were over.

Some evenings I went out with Ben for a cheap meal or just to the pub, once or twice to see a film. We talked about books, I suppose, and a little about work, and we talked about who was following him, because it was true – wher-ever we went, when we looked around, he was there. He wasn't just a character dreamt up in one of Ben's stories. A big man, a heavy man, which I said was to Ben's advantage, because if follow ever came to chase this was not a man who could move fast. Big, but not obviously threatening, except in the way he was always there. In his forties; not given to smiling, or to small talk either, and neatly though not showily dressed. There was no out-of-bounds, he was saying: we could slum it or posh it but he'd be tagging along. For me there was something entertaining as well as creepy about all this: at least someone was paying us atten-tion. Because of his size and his long sloping forehead I nicknamed him the Moose; Ben, who thought I was being flippant, didn't call him anything. Sometimes, in a pub or coming out of a cinema, I'd catch the Moose's eye and nod to him. It got to the stage of him nodding back.

Was he working for Bella? Bella surely knew who had taken her necklace. The scene she'd made in the hotel lobby must have been staged for Geoff, with Ben just a counter in a game she was playing, but still, it had been lousy of her to make that scene, to put the hotel chambermaids in the firing line, and to me this was a kind of relief: despite the gorgeous hair and all the other very evident attributes, if she was this kind of person I didn't want to know. Or was he working for Geoff? Ben thought that he was, and that his job prospects were now totally screwed. I told him Geoff was far too busy trying to salvage his own job or planning his exit route to worry about anything else. Besides, although he'd have liked the idea of having his own private detective, he wasn't that furtive. He was predictable, unimaginative; he liked his shiny car and his shiny new wife and any excuse for champagne. He was basically too slow on the uptake. In fact we were all a bit slow, apart from Ben himself on the night he passed by the open door. It was what we had in common, what buoyed us all up and, I see now, brought us all down. We were a species that failed to adapt.

The Moose, I reckoned, was simply a man who'd taken a fancy to Ben and who was becoming a little too obsessive, having decided that I was not a serious competitor. He was a stalker, not a hit-man. His intentions, however self-interested, were benign. He was probably lonely. I thought Ben was lonely too. Are mooses social animals? I never thought he was a bad person, or at least no worse than Ben or me, not that we set especially high standards. Ben, of course, disagreed; and it probably does feel different if you are the person being stalked rather than just watching the moves. I didn't press him. I was happy to have Ben staying on my couch but the possibility that despite the Bella episode he was gay was not my business. He might have asked my advice. I had none to offer. I was not, as they'd put it these days, his mentor. I didn't even ask him what he'd done with the necklace.

Usually the Moose would just appear in a pub soon after we'd settled in and stay until we left, hunched over his pint and an evening paper, but there came a night when he blinked first – I mean, he drained his glass and headed for the door while we were still talking. I can't blame him; we weren't giving him much reason to string along, and certainly no great nights out. As soon as he was out of the door, Ben tugged my sleeve and we set off in pursuit, turning the tables. It was raining and the streets were almost empty. The Moose stopped at a cash machine and we stopped too, maybe twenty yards away, but Ben made no attempt to disguise what we were doing and I knew then that I was the follower, the hanger-on, because Ben was on a high and had his own agenda.

The man turned left and walked down a cobbled alleyway that looked like a cul-de-sac, so we stood at the corner and watched. I was expecting him to enter one of the doors on either side but instead he unlocked a bike from a railing near the end and started cycling back up the alleyway. Just as he reached us Ben suddenly lunged towards him and shouted, and the bike skidded on the wet cobbles. The man fell off, hitting his head against the kerb. Then there were headlights, a car approaching, and Ben walked quickly away and I ran to catch up, but not before I'd noticed that one of the bicycle wheels was still turning but the Moose wasn't moving at all.

Ben moved out the next day, going back to his studio flat somewhere south of the river, taking his black jumpers with him and his two pairs of clumpy shoes and the second-hand typewriter on which he wrote his stories. Within weeks the office had closed and after that I never saw him again.

'Do you think he was mad?' Tom asked me. I'd assumed

that for Tom this was all in the archives, because he was a historian and it was his job to know these things, but he wasn't a historian now and maybe never had been, it was just the part we'd assigned him. He's a hotel-keeper. I discovered this last year, when I was down in Cornwall and someone recommended a hotel and when I arrived, there was Tom behind the bar. He greeted me as if I was coming into the pub after work, and he'd gone ahead to get in the first round. My meal that night was cooked by Tom's wife, a genial, bustling woman who ran from table to table making chirpy conversation. Tom was Tom, even more so than before (he'd put on weight): stolid, trustworthy, calm. They combined well. When the other guests at the hotel had retired to bed – these are quieter, more health-conscious days – Tom put a bottle of malt whisky on the bar and we talked. He showed me the photograph of us all lined up on the lawn and I told him about the time I had spent with Ben. It turned out he knew nothing.

No, not mad. Just back row, fourth from the right.

Geoff was somewhere in America, Tom told me, teaching at some small-town college in thrall to his English accent. Teaching what? He shrugged. And Bella? He shrugged again. All he knew was that Geoff had gone out there alone, and she hadn't followed him. I could probably find her on the internet, he said, if I was really curious. I wasn't.

Next morning, late down to breakfast in the dining room, I sat next to a group of around eight people, mostly women. They were, I picked up, all members of a painting class booked into the hotel for a week, and this was their last day. They were spinning out their meal, fidgeting and glancing out of the window – it had started to rain, grey clouds were blowing in, and it seemed unlikely they'd get to pitch their easels in front of whichever scenic view they'd had planned. Possibly none of them had known any of the others before the start of the week, but by now they were relaxed and familiar with each other's mannerisms, appetites, fronts. Roles had been taken up, or allotted: the joker, the organiser, the quiet one, the lazy one, the one to keep an eye on. I was starting to do this allotting myself, even though I'd been observing these people for less than half an hour. And as I poured coffee and munched toast, I remembered one of our last pub sessions together, before the office closed and we soldiered off, wending our separate ways into the unscripted future. We played a game that turned into a truth game, each of us telling the others where we saw them in ten years' time. We're all long past that deadline now. Someone, I can't recall who and I've no idea why this has stuck with me, told me I'd be a tree surgeon. Joyce could switch from bossy to easy-going and back to bossy without blinking, and I told her she'd be running a wine bar, with lock-ins on Friday nights. Her customers would both love her and know never to take advantage. In return, Joyce told me that if she ever came across a pile of neatly folded clothes on a beach, and footsteps in the sand leading into the sea but not out of it, she'd know whose those footsteps were. I told Ben that he'd be married to a primary school teacher in Hackney and running a little magazine from the spare bedroom, except that after they'd had their first child it wouldn't be spare any more. Either that or he'd pick up a brick one day and smash someone's head in and spend the rest of his life behind bars. One of the two.

A THURSDAY

Once or twice. She didn't like me, I could tell. You get used to that. How is she? Will she die?

Not long after he was arrested, the boy was in a room with a man who claimed to be a therapist, and because I was in the room too I heard the man ask him – they were talking about his childhood, the before time, before me – ask him this: 'So mothers are people who die?' So are psychotherapists. So are train drivers and shopkeepers. They don't choose to do this, usually. Sometimes it's just an accident. Sometimes another person chooses for them.

I know it's me he wanted to stick with the knife – from the kitchen drawer, by the way: was I supposed to padlock it? – but I walked out, I left them to it. That room was horrible and you could say it was painted in neutral colours but you'd be wrong, they were colour of vomit.

I never met his mother. I've seen photos. I think her dying abroad, while they were on holiday, meant that she hadn't *really* died. Like foreign money being Monopoly money, not real money. She'd just taken another holiday, a holiday from a holiday. He may have been expecting her to walk in through the door. On his birthday – if I were him, I'd have been expecting that.

Why shouldn't he have hated me? I came along, people do, and walked in. The door was open. The house was a big house. His father – but you know this – was not poor. You could be in that house and not know there was anyone else there. When his father wanted to know where he was, or wanted something from him, he had to shout. I never liked that. I did like the underfloor heating. You could walk around with just a T-shirt on as if it was summer, and it was winter outside, snow on the ground.

The boy is fifteen, his father is forty-six, I am close to the mid-point between them – but you have this on file. I like my coffee milky, two sugars, I have a problem with spiders, my favourite colour is blue, I had a bad experience with a maths teacher at school – what exactly do you need?

I do a lot of driving these days, to nowhere in particular. I mean at night. I don't like lying down, going to sleep, until I have no choice. Sometimes west, out of town, sometimes north, up the motorway. Nowhere is never nowhere. There's a 24-hour service station I've stopped at a few times in the early hours, enough to notice the regulars there. There's nothing odd about them, until you keep seeing them, and even then. I doubt I'd recognise them outside of that place, in their daily lives. We're ghosts. I have coffee, I sit for a while, I drive back. And that car . . . It's his father's car, an expensive car. Meaning it goes fast, if you want it to. But I don't – I'm a safe driver, I defer to to others, I've been driving for over ten years and never had an accident. They are lethal things, cars.

The flowers were not the first thing but everything followed from those. They were for my birthday. They were white. They were lovely. He'd trimmed them with a knife – from the drawer, maybe even the same one – and put them in a vase on the kitchen table and he was sweetness and light and this was to be a new beginning, and of course his father was pleased, proud, moved to tears. Whatever they were – whatever was in season, lilies, dahlias, I've no idea, I'm not good with flowers – they were expensive. Except of course he hadn't paid for them. Which he told me afterwards, which if I was keen on this sweetness-and-light thing I could never tell his father. That was the deal.

This is not an exculpation. Is that a word?

Shoplifting is hardly a crime, as these things go, but it is one. And maybe if you'd picked him up for that none of this would have happened. I'm just saying. He was lucky. Of course he had a talent too – he could be there and not there, he didn't attract notice – but it wasn't a career choice.

Books. Shoes. Flowers. Soap. *Things* – and why not, I thought. The books were easy, because no one was keeping an eye out, no one was interested, they were just clocking time. They don't employ graduates in that shop, graduates steal books. And the shoes – you know how they display only one of a pair, so there's no point stealing them? Well, he did. Bless him. I mean that. Bags of nails from the hardware shop, lightbulbs, a tape measure. Magazines, literary ones, high-brow – his father was impressed by those, and by the condoms too, he had a son who was responsible and mature and grown-up, who was finding his own way in the world, who would have made his mother proud.

I don't think the condoms got used. And the magazines – well, art, politics, with those you can't do it alone, you have to join someone's gang and then you lose control, don't you?

When you're an only child and you're angry, you have no one to take it out on except yourself. And the world in general, of course. There is that. He'd been hurt, and stealing was a way of getting back. He was bad, he'd let his mother die and he'd let her be replaced by me, and stealing is what bad people do. The touch of genius was to turn me, his enemy, into his collaborator, so we could be bad people together.

The soap – I washed myself with it. Scented soap. There was a vanilla one that his father liked too, liked on my skin I mean. The boy had – has – good taste. There is a woman out there who may still be a lucky woman. There's plenty left, a drawerful, a bigger drawer than the knife drawer, more than I can use. Do you want some?

There was a scarf too. Ladies and gentlemen, we give you the boy wizard, the magician who can conjure silk scarves from nowhere. *And his glamorous assistant* – see him fold her into a box and saw her in half, see him tie her to the wall with ribbons and throw knives at her. See her step free, so he can do it all over again.

Tell me one thing, *one thing*, you can't read something sexual into.

I ironed his T-shirts, I folded them, I read the slogans. *Dead on arrival* – was that one meant for me? A lot of washing goes on in a house with a family inside it, even if it's not really a family. Washing, then drying, then sorting, then ironing. It's continuous. I'm not complaining. It's something you do, and then it's done. And if something goes wrong – but the washing machine was insured, he was big on insurance, the boy's father. Not just the usual house-and-contents but the individual appliances, the pipe-work, the gadgets, no gap in the defences. Enough small print to keep you in reading for six months, and you'd be no wiser. It's a form of betting, I know, almost you *want* something to go wrong so you can collect your winnings. The boy had private health insurance. *I* was insured. I still am, I'd guess. Everything was on direct debit, automatic. If I crashed the car and lost an arm or a leg, there'd be a paying out. Except of course if the accident was due to an act of God. The insurance companies are big on God, it's in their interest that God exists and his behaviour remains as it's always been, which is fickle. He keeps them in business. The get-out clause.

I'm wandering. But I was wandering then, we all were, and none of us was stupid. It's what you do, until this happens, and then you start doing it again. We were blind, me included, but his father especially. Money makes you go blind. Did you know that?

I was unsettled – more than that: I hadn't seen this in him, or if I had I'd shut my eyes – by how easily his father was taken in, by how important it was to him that his son read those magazines. Said please and thank you, didn't swear, that his son should be a credit to himself – it meant he'd been right all along, in his choices, never made a mistake. I, of course, was one of his choices.

I do this or I do that . . . It probably averages out, fifty-fifty. It's just that I don't need other people to validate my choices, it's not what they're there for.

Hindsight, now there's a word. I think, in the end, and maybe even in the beginning too, the boy wanted me to tell him, his father. I've thought about this when I'm driving, looking into the windows of houses. Not all the time. Usually I'm thinking why do they need such a big TV, what I'm going to eat tomorrow, the little things. I narrow down to what's in front of me. You see more foxes in town than you do when you get into the countryside.

You know how when you're driving on a motorway there are times you get stuck in the fast lane and you can't get back into the middle lane? You know how when you're talking to someone who knows your name and you've forgotten theirs but after a certain time it's too late to admit this, to ask? It was all happening so quickly, and at the same time in slow motion, like I was watching it but couldn't change it.

I saw his father one morning – the car must have been at the garage – getting onto the boy's bike. It was cold, he was well wrapped-up, he jabbed a half-cigar into his mouth, lit up, stepped onto the bike and rode off, and there was a bag hanging from the handlebars and written on it was 'I Love My Toys'.

'You want something from me,' he once said to me. I wasn't sure that I did, any longer. 'Can't you just love me?' he asked. It's not as complicated as that.

I have had this conversation so many times.

If I'm tired when I'm driving at night, back from the service station, or just around, I talk to myself. It's a sign of sanity. I used to imagine the boy was in the back seat, or sometimes his father, and I'd open up a conversation. But neither of them had much to say. So now it's usually some hitch-hiker I've picked up. Not a real one, of course – it's not something people do these days, they think they're going to get raped or killed and thrown in a ditch – but one who still believes other people are basically decent and kind. I ask them about their lives. Not all of them want to talk, some of them close their eyes and fall asleep or pretend to fall asleep, but you hear some amazing things.

The woman in the hardware shop? Because she'd been watching him, because he'd been getting careless, over-confident, because she knew who he was and she knew his father too and she'd tell him – that's why her. I can't prove it. Beause she was wearing a red dress. Because there was no one else in the shop, because it was raining, because he knew this had to end at some time and he was getting bored. Because he'd skipped breakfast. Because it was a Thursday. Because somewhere in outer Mongolia a butterfly flapped its wings. You choose.

Boys – men – don't have *accessories*. OK, maybe iPhones, headphones. Maybe he wanted something to go with his jeans that day. Maybe the knife just felt right. They put her age in brackets, I noticed that.

My driving license, yes. By the way, I never smoke in that car, I never leave my wrappers on the seat, I keep it clean. If he wants it back all he has to do is say. You want to see my *driving license*?

Like buses or big lorries when they're turning: you give them space, you let them into your own lane, then you move on. I don't know *what* this is like, but as I said, I do a lot of driving these days and things come into my head, unconnected things, but they're crying out to be connected. It's like the economy, everything is linked to everything else, you change the interest rates and people lose jobs and inflation goes up or goes down, I don't know, and if that doesn't work you do something else. I didn't pay for the car, and I don't pay for the insurance either, but the price of petrol is ridiculous. It creeps up, in a way you don't notice, or try not to notice. I'm sure his father doesn't notice.

PETER WAS IN PARIS

Peter was in Paris. Ben, unless he was with Peter, was in Bonn. Mohammed was in the Maldives. The world was their board game: they made their moves and took up positions and second-guessed the others.

Caroline was at home.

'God,' said Peter from Paris. 'What did you say her name was?'

'Amira.'

A pause. He had no idea, or he knew very well but it was too complicated to explain on the phone.

'Tell her to come to the house. She can stay a few nights, can't she? I'll be back by the weekend.'

She had already done so. The girl was sitting with her now: nineteen, the age when nothing is not funny or exciting, exactly as her voice had been on the phone from Heathrow: 'I'm so happy, so happy. Where is Peter?' She was not just devastatingly pretty, she was flawless. Her luggage, piled in the hall, indicated more than a fleeting visit. There would be trouble; arrangements would need to be made.

~

Her first time in London, yes. But she had been to

America, to Washington. Her father was a Jordanian dip-
lomat, perhaps an ambassador. She had an older brother
who had come to London to study medicine but had disappeared, no one had heard from him for two years. She mentioned an American boy three times; the first time he was
a boyfriend, the second just a boy, the third he could have
been either. It was hard to know what was true and what
was made up, but in the end Caroline decided to believe
everything she was told, even if it was contradictory, which
was the policy she adopted with Peter.

Peter this, Peter that. He had been very kind. Something
about getting her into a certain school, after problems at a
previous one – Peter was returning a favour that her father,
the ambassador, had done for him, she understood this, but
really he had gone to so much trouble, talked to so many
people. He was so generous. He was special. Had Caroline
been married to Peter for long? He had often spoken about
her. That, surely, was made up.

'Oh, a long time,' Caroline said. She didn't quite want
to say: 'Since I was your age, roughly. Since I was young.'

Though given the amount of time that Peter spent
abroad, and always had done, perhaps not that long after
all.

Peter was the world's leading authority on the history
and politics of Saudi Arabia. This was her tease. He happened to have done some travelling, and to speak Arabic,
and to have worked in banking in the Middle East, and
along the way he had made enough contacts to estab-
lish himself as an 'expert'. His opinions were paid for; he
attended conferences in America, Singapore; when something happened – an assassination, a hike in the market for
crude oil – the BBC got in touch. He was lean and tanned,
like an explorer. The cameras liked him. He, in turn, liked

women but was only ever truly relaxed with other men. And when the chips were down, when the knives came out, Caroline knew that the only people he trusted were his team, his improbable blood-brothers: Ben, who was young and blond and blue-eyed but too spoiled, too chubby, to be handsome; and Mohammed, a grey-faced older Egyptian with a beard and sad, watery eyes. The three musketeers. Like the royal family, they were rarely ever together in the same place at the same time.

On Thursday Caroline took Amira on the train into town and they went on the Millennium Wheel and looked out over the whole of London, or as far as the mist allowed. Back on solid ground, Amira's hand – soft and surprisingly warm – sought out Caroline's, and they walked along the riverbank like sisters. Caroline herself had never been to the Globe Theatre before. Bits of Shakespeare came back to her, but it didn't seem the right place or time, even though it was exactly both. She apologised for the weather, the cold.

'Oh, it's what I expected,' Amira said. 'I mean, this is London.' She laughed. Caroline liked her, despite wondering what else she had expected.

Not sisters – they might be mother and daughter, the daughter coming home for a spell after a row with her boyfriend, not knowing what to do with her life. Caroline would listen, into the small hours; she was a good listener. There would be confessions and tears and slow hugs, and after the girl went away again, as she must, they would write letters to each other, like people used to, full of gossip and jokey put-downs of Peter. Through the months, the seasons, Caroline would describe the garden, what had come up well and what hadn't.

On the phone, Peter was effusive and grateful. He'd be

back when? It might take a bit longer, Mohammed had arrived in town and they had people to see. 'And you have a girl waiting for you here,' Caroline told him. 'A girl who's not used to being kept waiting.' 'I'm sure you'll find ways to entertain her,' Peter said. They were bantering. The line was bad, there was background noise.

But the next day was more difficult. It rained continuously; there was a constant splattering on the gravel outside the front window, from where the gutter hadn't been cleared of last autumn's leaves. Normally, on her own, Caroline would have had the radio on and might not have even heard this, but today she did. In the afternoon they went to the cinema in the local town centre; an old man, perhaps drunk, snored in the row behind them; each time Caroline turned round and prodded his knees he stopped but then would start again, and Amira giggled.

Afterwards, in the car on the way home, she talked about one of the actors in the film and said she had met him, in America. Had Caroline met him?

Caroline said she didn't know any actors. Or singers, come to that. She had once met Tony Blair's wife at a charity event.

'But Peter knows him,' said Amira. 'He introduced us.' She was looking out of the car window at the rain-soaked verges, the derelict petrol station, the place run by the mildewed woman that took in pets when their owners went on holiday. 'Peter knows everyone. He should write a book.'

There was in fact a book. Lying on Peter's desk at home was the manuscript of the autobiography of a Saudi minister, though the words in English were Peter's. He had told her the outline: born in a tent in the desert, the minister now lived in a palace with golden taps, and was blind and dying, and Peter would arrange for private publication so that the man's life would exist as a book and could be sent to his daughters in America, his daughters who even as they'd been chauffeured to the airport to embark on their expensive foreign education had already known that they'd never return to Arabia.

In all of history it had rarely been possible to make this journey from tent to palace in the span of one lifetime, and most of those who had achieved this were tyrants, and perhaps it never would be possible gain.

While Caroline made supper, Amira turned the pages. From the kitchen, Caroline heard occasional laughter. Then the TV was switched on.

Caroline too had turned the pages. She had agreed to edit this book, but it was so appallingly written it was irredeemable. Time had flown too fast. Fact played too easily into bad fiction and a level of understanding, of basic curiosity – why would anyone *want* their taps made of solid gold? – had been missed out.

She chopped onions and garlic and browned the meat, and when the rice was on she poured wine. 'Is it French?' the girl asked. It was from Waitrose. When Caroline asked what kind of food her mother cooked at home, the girl said that her mother didn't cook. She understood that Amira came from a wealthy family and had probably never in her life made her own bed, washed up or stooped to pick fluff from the floor. Nor did she appear to have any concept of privacy.

Later, after supper, Caroline phoned Peter, who didn't answer, and left a message: she was coming to Paris and bringing Amira with her. Then she called the hotel and booked a room.

~

They checked in – a room with twin beds – and Caroline lay down, exhausted by what she had done. Peter wasn't there; a room was still reserved in his name but from the discreet replies of the staff at the reception desk she gathered it hadn't been used for two nights. But the girl was unfailing. 'Where are we?' she asked, opening on the bed next to Caroline the city plan she had picked up at reception. The Tour Eiffel, the Louvre, Versailles – her eyes were lit up. The map crinkled; it would be difficult to fold back. She traced the streets with her long fingers. She wanted to set off immmediately.

Caroline let her. Amira had not come here to be chaperoned.

Late in the afternoon she woke up, cold and still fully dressed. She had dreamt but could remember nothing; she felt there was something in her mouth that needed chewing, something gristly, but however long she chewed it would never break up and and at some point she would just have to swallow. She drew the room curtains, showered and brushed her teeth, and went out.

The sun had already set but the lights in the shops in the streets around the hotel were low. High fashion, beyond mortal purses. A book and print shop: a man wearing thick glasses and a thin, pale woman sat at a table inside, plotting, like characters in one of the leather-bound books on the shelves around them; in the window, engraved maps of Paris in the eighteenth century. The streets were quiet; this was not the tourist season, neither the new year nor spring. No one was buying. These were not shops, they were fronts for something else.

She felt a kind of despair. She felt that she was being watched, or that a toxic drug was being dispersed through the chill, damp mist that rose off the river and threaded through the streets. Peter had probably not got her message, in which case no one in the world, apart from Amira, knew where she was. A woman on the pavement in front of her dragging a tiny dog on a lead suddenly slipped and fell, as if shot down by a rooftop sniper. Caroline helped her up; the woman seemed to push her away, the dog bared its teeth and growled. This, in a window displaying oriental antiques, was hideous: a squat Cambodian god of heavy stone, seated cross-legged, anonymous, around three feet high. Its hat or hair was a cartoonish topknot. It seemed a concentration of evil. Its presence here was a corruption, though it would never, now, move. It was too dense, too leaden. If a nuclear bomb annihilated the whole of the city, this would remain. She couldn't bear to look into its dead stone eyes; equally she couldn't look away.

She recalled certain pages from the typescript of the blind Saudi minister's book. It might even sell a few copies, Peter had said: dying, with nothing to lose, the minister had felt free to relate the antics of the playboy princelings on their jaunts to this very city. Not a sexual show-and-tell, more an accounts sheet: amounts of money, addresses, numbers of girls, numbers of boys. Everyone knew but no one before had spelt it out in such detail. It was all, Caroline decided, compared with the ageless malevolence of the stone god and the cruelty of the hereditary high priests, trivial, even innocent.

Back at the hotel, Caroline went directly to the bar. Rows of bottles glinted in the light from an open fire. She deserved this. The warmth brought blood back to her face.

The man seated with his back to her was Peter. Opposite, facing her, from a deep sofa Amira glanced up and joyfully exclaimed. There were others – an older woman with amused, intelligent eyes, two men who might have been military, and bearded Mohammed, who rose and kissed her hand like a courtier from a previous century. They were drinking Champagne.

Peter stood up and drew her in. He and Mohammed had found Amira in the street, dressed far too lightly for this winter afternoon, standing outside a Metro station and turning her map until it might chance to make sense.

'Peter rescued me,' Amira said.

'Not that you needed rescuing,' said Peter.

'Yes, I did. That boy, he was following me all the way –'

The older woman caught the eye of a waiter, ordering more Champagne. Caroline looked at Peter, who was delighted. This was what he was for, rescuing people, and the girl had made it so easy.

They squashed into two taxis and went to a restaurant, which appeared to be expecting them. Caroline carried on drinking, at first because she was still cold and then because she wasn't, and besides, having delivered the girl, she had nothing else to do, she was free. The restaurant was in a basement.

With all the noise and the carelessness, they might have been celebrating something, and perhaps they were. There were more people around the table than there had been at the hotel but they were all, in a way that didn't bear questioning, family. They spoke in English and French and Arabic; their voices overlapped and then rang clear and then overlapped again, like the lights of traffic at night circling the Arc de Triomphe. Peter had his arm around Amira's bare shoulders. On the way in, in the crush to go downstairs, he had whispered in Caroline's ear that there was nothing, nothing in the world, that had not been possible but for her, and to cut through the double negatives she had kissed him. Now the woman with amused eyes, seated directly opposite Caroline, was trying to talk to her about Proust, and then about gardening. When the floor show began Amira became restless: she wanted to dance, and it was clear to Caroline that she would do so better than any of the paid performers and that neither Peter nor any of the others would stop her.

The person she felt watching her was Mohammed, and she looked into his eyes and was surprised to see the desert there, where she had expected money. But not white dunes under an azure sky. A rocky, inhospitable landscape. The world's great religions had come out of such places, and no wonder, they were so bleak, so ravaged.

'Where's Ben?' she asked.

'He's in Bahrain.'

She had to laugh.

Peter laughed with her, and then the girl too, Amira, who couldn't possibly have known what what the joke was and it was barely a joke anyway, it wouldn't bear explaining. But she had spirit, and she would outlast them all. Caroline reached out and placed her hand on Mohammed's wrist, and he smiled – she had never once seen him laugh, in the way the others did – and he didn't withdraw.

LIVES OF THE
ARTISTS

They sat in the café on the fourth floor of Tate Modern. They had spent an hour in the exhibition and the stuffing had been knocked out of them. It was rush hour in there, it was Waterloo station, it was Heathrow on a bank holiday when the flights have been delayed. Between wall-to-wall shoulders, they had glimpsed masterpieces.

'Does no one have any work to go to?' asked Clare, annoyed with herself for having taken off a fine, bright, breezy afternoon and then spent it failing to look at art. She had the stubs of their tickets in her hand. Would he claim them on expenses? 'But thank you. These weren't cheap.'

'Here's what we do next time,' said Ryan, whose hourly rate was many hundreds of pounds and who had unilaterally decided that there was going to be a next time. She could choose to resent this; she hadn't made up her mind. 'If we go in through the exit, there's often no one there to check the tickets.'

'That's cheating.'

'And the artist wouldn't cheat? There were times when he couldn't afford a roll of canvas and a decent brush.'

'But then you get everything backwards.'

'You do. First off, the late, great paintings. The hard-won

freedom. All the labour and struggle have been distilled out.'

'Like one of those board games – jump forward ten squares.'

'You move against the crowd. You sidestep through the doorways and use the space that's always left between the paintings and where people stand to look at them. Like a corridor. People get annoyed but usually they just move on. The years of fame: prizes, travel, the record auction prices, the ex-wives –'

'How many?'

'Definitely plural. They changed their women like they changed their styles, their agents, their galleries.'

'Except the ones who died young.'

'They fitted a lot in. They were in a hurry. But we're through to the middle rooms now: dealers, patrons, affairs, alcohol. The trademark style, the four-year block.'

'Snakes and ladders.'

'Keep walking. The apprenticeship: art school, politics, influences, girlfriends.'

'There's always a room with *brown* paintings –'

'Brown and small. The colours have faded. At the time they went for a song – if your great-grandfather had picked one up –'

'Maybe he did?'

'Don't linger. Smile at the gallery assistants checking the tickets of the people coming in and out you go.'

'Past the shop.'

'The shop?'

'Postcards, T-shirts, key rings –'

'We've got no money, remember? Or not enough for a ticket. Just keep on going.'

'Where to?'

'Before there were any paintings. Before a hand reached out for a brush. Just the itch of ambition, inarticulate rebellion –'

'Dish-washing in a hotel in the middle of nowhere. I did that.'

'Boredom, rejection, neglect, all the way back to the source of the Nile –'

'A muddy trickle –'

'The womb.'

Later – on a bus: she'd insisted on it – Clare realised that the sleek retrospective logic offered by the reverse route was deceptive. There was no absolute reason why the work in room 5, for example, should have followed the work in room 4. At the next junction, the bus she was on could turn left, could turn right, could veer past the church and go straight on. He just wanted to get her into bed.

∽

Ryan: mid-fifties, a lawyer (commercial law), recently become a widower, and not a hundred per cent sure that the woman he was sitting opposite was in fact Clare – a woman he'd known at college, three decades and longer ago, a woman he hadn't seen since but whom out of the blue he had, for reasons mysterious to himself, but not *that* mysterious, made contact with and invited to see some Kandinskys. They might as well have been Kokoschkas. The point was, a neutral venue, a whiff of culture, the life of the mind for starters. There are wardens in every room, watching over: don't touch, don't touch. You buy the catalogue but are under no obligation to read the essays. You can get by very easily on Correggio, after being paid fifty crowns in copper coins for a painting on a hot summer day, joyously setting out to walk home to his wife – but 'the burthen, the walk, and the weather, threw him into a pleurisy, of which he died at 40 years old, anno 1513'. On Turner arguing with his patron about whether carrots float in water (they do), on Jackson Pollock being no mean hand at baking bread and pies. These tidbits – and tidbits, Ryan had already found out, were Clare's line – are a common currency. They tell you that artists are you or me, more or less. They strike lucky, or they don't. They like money and they like getting into places for free. They like sitting around having drunk or stoned conversations about whether carrots float. They need to eat.

The tickle of doubt, which he didn't dislike, the tiny per-centage, derived from the long-ago afternoon when he'd invited Clare for tea and a walk in his college gardens. The edges of the grass were neatly cut, without anyone ever being seen to cut them. Clare, blonde, spent most of her days – and her nights too, it was rumoured, but he didn't believe it – in company with her best friend, Helena, a redhead. He really should have been prepared for Clare to arrive with Helena in tow, but he wasn't, and because he was annoyed, and most likely hungover too, he paid attention less to Clare than to her chaperone, who turned out to be well-read and far from stupid (chaperones are people in whom other people place trust). Helena really wasn't interested in how pretty the daffodils were looking that afternoon. Helena had a mind of her own, and a body too, he noticed. Clare had flounced off, and Ryan had found himself hoping that if boredom drove her not just away but back the chaperone would have a bag of stale of bread with which the maiden could go and feed the ducks.

He had slept with Helena. He had also slept with Clare – twice, arguably three times (the third time may have been just that, an argument). And though it was Clare he had researched on the net – she ran a catering company, providing food themed to the client's whim – and it was Clare he'd invited to the Tate, the woman who came had deep brown hair, neither blonde nor red, and it was possible that he had misremembered. That whole period, looking back, was a laboured Shakespearian comedy in which characters dress up as other characters, or a costume drama set in a time when there were more rules, more etiquette, which itself is an item of female attire, an additional layer of underwear with a thousand tiny buttons. It didn't matter. This woman who had arrived, he would phone her that night, he would see her again. He did know that mistaken identity is the kind of error for which a lawyer can get sacked on the spot, and no woman forgives.

~

'How you doing, Clare? You good?' Jonny's voice on the phone made her go dizzy, so that she had to close her eyes and draw breath before answering, and by then he was speaking again and their words tangled.

'You'll come?'

He always gave her the option of saying no. He had a flat somewhere south of the river, but that was his studio. He had given her, pressed upon her, the key; he had nothing to hide. Most of the time he lived in a room in a friend's flat in east London. Sometimes he stayed over with Clare but never for longer than a couple of nights. He was lean and wandering, he skimmed the surfaces. He was using her. Of course she would go.

On Sunday afternoon she took the Tube and then a bus and then walked, and got lost in a housing estate. In a street of industrial buildings, most of which were now flats, she saw people standing around on the pavement with beer bottles in their hands. Jonny was among them. She walked towards him, and as she came close he turned towards her – not having watched her approach, just knowing she'd be there when he turned. He didn't kiss her. She'd said no to kissing in public. He was half her age; people assumed she was his mother; there were standards. The first time she'd said that, he'd laughed and told her she was the prime minister addressing the nation. What he did was duck his head to her neck, to the hollow above her collarbone, and then whisper in her ear.

He showed her his work inside the gallery, three small paintings of a child, a young boy, kneeling – praying? begging? – in what might have been a park. They were accomplished and gave nothing away; they were figurative paintings of a kind she'd thought was extinct, which surprised her. It was like being introduced to someone's parents. She didn't know what to say. Crushing Jonny's hand in hers, she said they were great. But those weren't his paintings – he had misled her, or among the babble of voices around them she'd misunderstood. *This* was his work. They were standing in front of what appeared to be an architect's blueprints, lines and perfect curves and text in tiny print. If she looked more closely, it was possible she might see into his mind. To her side, a black cloth was hung across a doorway; she parted the curtain and stepped through.

Two videos were being projected onto precariously balanced screens. As her eyes adjusted to the darkness, she saw figures moving in slow motion, careful not to stumble over cables on the floor. There was a soft whirring that perhaps might never end. After a week in this room, she thought, all things would be well. Then someone was standing behind her, his hands – she was sure it was a he – cupping her breasts. She took a long breath but she didn't cry out because she thought this might be part of the show. She walked outside, blinking in the sunshine, and found Jonny back on the pavement with a group of others, drinking beer.

'Hey, Clare.' The way he kept using her name sometimes made her giddy with happiness, as if she'd just been unwrapped, a present to herself. He told her that the owner of the gallery – he pointed towards a small man who looked like a cab driver – had offered him a solo show. He was grinning, and possibly drunk.

He was taking the place of someone who'd been going to show in a couple of months' time but had pulled out.

When would he do the work? How would he pay for the materials?

He shrugged and pulled her to him, wrapping her so closely she could feel the jut of his bones.

She was a fool, a fool for love, all her friends told her – caringly, cloyingly, with a suspicious unanimity. Any election won by a unanimous vote must be rigged.

On Monday morning she woke to find him standing at the foot of the bed, already dressed, looking at her intently as if she was something he'd just made. She gave him her credit card and told him to go to an artists' supplies place, and though she got the card back in the post she didn't see Jonny for another three months.

～

The countryside, even at its furthest edges, is not more restful, not more quiet, than the city. Even with the window closed she could hear the sea, its continuous roll and drag on the pebbly beach.

On the stand on Ryan's side of the bed there was a book, a novel, with a bookmark trapped between its pages. In the bathroom, six towels, two razors, two toothbrushes, his and hers; in the wardrobe, more clothes than anyone might need for a weekend. Before you know it, there is barely room to move.

When Ryan reached for the book she put a hand on his shoulder to stop him. He looked at her, waiting, and she told him a story, the story of Jonny – from the day when he had come into her life from behind, by speeding up and then adjusting his pace to hers and walking alongside and telling her that she had good legs. She'd been on her way to order quail's eggs for a hundred canapés, or maybe two hundred, and she was forty-seven and it was six years since anyone had remarked on her legs and that whole thing had been a mess she counted herself lucky to escape alive from. But on the evening of the next day Jonny, dressed as a nineteenth-century midshipman and with his hair tied in a pigtail, was moving smoothly around a room of chattering people with trays of finger-food. *Navigating* – the party was for a shipping company. Latitude and longitude, the precise location where two glances intersect; they joked about this later, the magnetic pole. His trays emptied faster than those of the other servers combined. Flirting, but getting away with it because he did so from below decks, he placed a quail's egg between the lips of the woman who wore the most strapless dress in the room. With his other hand he held a wide tray in perfect balance.

Ryan nodded. He stroked the side of her forehead, smoothing back her hair. She turned away, offering him the other side, and he stroked again.

Clare had a thing about balance. She was well known in her trade for her menus, which took in savoury and sweet, sweet and sour, and exact proportions of all those vitamins and proteins that are said to be essential. But it was more than that. It was bordering on obsessive-compulsive. If she was in a hurry, and somehow bashed her elbow or kicked her own ankle, she had to knock the other elbow or ankle too, inflicting as far as possible exactly the same degree of pain. And then the first one again, if she'd overdone it. She had once read – and had remembered for ever after – that the right side of the brain was creativity, intuition, magic, and the left side was logic, planning, lists.

'It's the other way round,' Ryan said.

Maybe he was right. It was confusing. The right-hand side of the brain controlled the left-hand side of the body. Jonny was left-handed.

He also had one eyebrow that was completely white. People's hair can be turned white overnight, legend has it, by a traumatic experience. Often in a war, but there is always a war. She didn't ask, and anyway he covered his tracks. Jonny was not his real name, which was unpronounceable, he claimed, being Serbian, or Bulgarian. He was neither of those things; his skin was too dark. Yet when he said he was an artist, Clare had believed him, perhaps because of that eyebrow.

Ryan said that this boy, this Jonny, was two-a-penny. They come up to you while you're sitting outside Starbucks and bum a cigarette or the price of a drink – you say no, and no again, and they say 'Because it's so exhausting?', and because they are intelligent and clearly, you can tell from their faces, deserve to live, you give in. Or you don't, and as they walk off they mutter something about your meanness, your selfishness, and you reply that if they'd bother to stick around they'd find you can be a lot more selfish and petty than that, which was just for starters, but they've gone now, out of hearing. Or a girl shouts across the road to a boy – this had happened to him only last week – for what time it is and he ignores her, so you tell her yourself and now you're stuck with her, and she's not interested in what time it is at all but she has a history with that boy which she tells you, in a druggy kind of way. Other lives. It's what cities are for, it's why you choose to live there.

'And why sometimes you choose to get out,' he added, 'for weekends in the country.'

'What do they want, these people?' Clare asked, as if she really didn't know, and if he couldn't give better than the answers that everyone gives – money, love – she'd never speak to him again.

'Will you marry me?' Ryan replied.

For a lawyer, she told him, playing for time, he asked surprisingly few questions.

∼

She came across Jonny walking down Bond Street wearing orange trousers and an eye-mask over his eyes, the kind they give out on long-haul flights, business class, so you can rest your eyes from looking out of the window at the sublime, the pinks or the yellows or golds of nothing but sky, depending on the hour of the day, and sometimes a billowy layer of cloud, which becomes unbearable after a time, and he was holding a white stick in front of him and moving it from side to side as if sweeping for landmines or scattering seed. People made way, let him carve his own path. He was, he said, after they'd sat down and he'd removed his mask, placing it on the table between them, making love to the world.

What blindfolds are for, he told her, is to increase the pleasure of erotic play – the other senses shift up a gear to compensate. And his walking along the street was, in case she hadn't noticed, performance art. She looked at him over the café table and thought how young he looked and was, a free agent without history or attachments. The comparison with Ryan was unfair; but he was, still, lovely. And you do have to decide, when you go into town and drift among the art galleries and the commercial offices, often jostling for space on the same street, whether this is for real or that, or which you want more.

'Have you ever been to Venice?' she asked him.

It rained; they were marooned, shipwrecked. Jonny sulked. Just as you can work up an interest in art, so you can work up a complete indifference to it, or scorn. Art doesn't mind. They stood together in front of Giorgione's *The Tempest* in the Accademia and he asked the questions a child asks, a difficult, precocious child in a room full of grown-ups. A woman under a tree, breastfeeding an infant, is wearing nothing but a white and flimsy cloth around her shoulders – didn't she feel the cold? Was the climate warmer in olden times? It's night-time – a moon floats behind the clouds – so why is everything so bright?

There's a crack of lightning in the sky; the noise of thunder will follow, and pouring rain, and both the woman and the man will get soaking wet. In the foreground of the painting, on the left, a man stands holding a long wooden stick and ogling the woman. A macho pose: elbow thrust out, one leg bent at the knee, the other leg straight. He is young, and always will be.

Clare fitted the bits together – while knowing that, by

taking the narrative line, by taking the difficult child at face value, she was laying herself open. The woman, out walking with her child, has been surprised by a thunderstorm. The baby is frightened and hungry, and the woman takes shelter under a tree on the riverbank, hoping the storm will soon pass. That was stupid, Jonny said – the lightning could strike the tree and it would crash down and kill them both. The man with the long stick is a passing soldier, a merce- nary, Clare said, and he's planning to attack the woman. Did he want to steal the child? Jonny asked. No, he just wanted to attack her. Why? Why did he think, she replied.

A woman – an Italian woman, of roughly the same age as the woman in the picture – had joined them and was listening. No, she said. She spoke English like the people at the reception desk in the hotel where they were staying, but from the way she was dressed she could have owned that hotel. She said the woman was a queen and the child was the heir to the throne and the man was her lover. He was keeping watch, protecting her.

And then Jonny was speaking to the woman in fluent Italian, a talent that up to then he'd kept hidden – how many more did he have? Russian, Arabic, besides Serbo- Croat or Bulgarian? Accountancy? Seamanship: he'd already been a mishipman. He could do anything, but now Clare felt brushed out, overpainted, and she suggested they go to the café. He told her to go ahead, said he'd follow her. She found her way down to the toilets, down a long corri- dor; it could easily have been a dungeon. An ancient crone sat knitting beside a small table on which there was a white saucer with coins and crumpled banknotes. The crone was as dry as those wafery banknotes, combustible, despite the sounds of water – trickling, flushing – around them; she could burst into flames at any moment. She probably lived there, in one of the cubicles. She scowled, witch-like, casting a spell on Clare as she scurried past, both going in and coming out.

There was no sign of Jonny in the café. Clare returned to the gallery but he wasn't there either, and neither was the Italian woman. She looked back at the painting as if that was where he had gone, hiding somewhere among the trees.

~

She had the key, the key to the flat he used as a studio. A tab to get into the building, a separate door key – she held them in her open palm.

She'd barely slept. Too much food, too much wine, and Ryan hadn't come to bed. In the early light flooding in through the uncurtained window of the living room he lay asleep on the long white sofa, stretched out on his back, shoes kicked off, his pale skin showing above his socks, and it struck her that he might be dead, because this was exactly how he'd be laid out on the ferry to the underworld.

One candle was still guttering. She pinched it out, then wiped her fingers gently on the sleeve of Ryan's shirt, leaving two murky smudges. He didn't stir. Ryan's flat was the opened-out top floor of a warehouse high above the river. He'd bought it for a song, way under the market price; she'd told him that he'd be lucky to get even that for it now but he said she hadn't factored in the Qataris. She looked down from the window at the river, the river running by.

Jonny's studio was on the sixth floor of a housing association block in Brixton. Changing from one Tube line to another, she trekked through underground passages lined with film posters: love, war, horror. Of course the lift was out of order. As she went up the stairs she saw herself as a character in a film, a thriller, something noir, whose audience – but not the character herself – expects someone to be waiting behind the door with an axe, or a body on the kitchen floor with a pool of blackened blood under its head.

There was neither. Instead there was a fair-haired boy of perhaps twelve sitting at a table, and there was music coming from a radio, popular music but not loud, some tinny sound, the volume turned down. The boy glanced at Clare as she came in and then carried on with what he was doing, which was drawing a picture – a picture of a very simple house, or a very simple picture of a house, so simple that it looked like the drawing of a five-year-old rather than a boy of eleven or twelve: a door, windows on either side and above, an angled roof. There was no attempt at perspective; really it was just a front wall.

She stood behind the boy and asked: 'Does the house have a garden?' The boy shook his head. He was shading in the roof. She noticed that he was copying the house from a book lying open in front of him, a children's book. 'What about some birds?' she asked, and he began adding birds in the sky, birds that were out of all proportion to the house because he was determined to get both wings in.

She lay down on the bed, which was just a mattress on a low base, listening to the music. The flat was basic: a studio room with bed, table and a kitchen range, a tiny bathroom. It was spotlessly clean. There were no canvases, no paint spills on the floor.

And then someone called from outside this clean, barely lived-in flat, a woman's voice, and the boy put his pencil down neatly on the table, turned off the radio and left.

Through the window she watched planes passing from

right to left, one every few minutes, climbing steeply, on a flight path out from the city airport, each one packed with you and me in rows. Soon there would be no one left in the city except herself and the boy, and they would live together in this flat for ever and a day, or if not that long then at least until the boy was old enough to forage for himself.

Are you happy? Jonny had once asked her. Not Ryan. Her answer would not be taken down in evidence. As happy as can be.

She stood up and looked at the book the boy had been copying from, turning the pages: an igloo, a teepee, a house on a canal, a house built around a courtyard. Houses of the world. Ryan knew about houses – he did the legal work for property developers, holding them back to the letter of the law, and the spirit too if it was convenient. Houses were his bread and butter and for a decade they'd been his jam too. Clare didn't know a thing about houses; for her they were just places with kitchens. But she noticed that the house the boy had drawn was not really like the one in the book at all. He was copying very badly, or he was making it up and just pretending to be copying. It was, she decided, a halfway house, a halfway house being a place of temporary refuge for those who are neither insane enough to be confined in a closed institution nor well-adjusted enough to be allowed to roam the streets. A halfway house being exactly halfway between hell and heaven, between the abyss and whatever is its opposite.

There are maps: she could find one.

Or it was a safe house, another place where people at risk are sheltered. This one is shielded by a barrier of codes and ciphers, by people being deliberately kept in ignorance. But ignorance is not secure, a little knowledge always seeps through and no safe house is safe for long. There are unannounced arrivals in the night, abrupt departures. Headlights sweep the drive.

EARLY MODERN

A drink, why not. He shouldn't have agreed. He shouldn't have taken the job, shouldn't have come back, and he shouldn't have said what he said but he did. These are the kind of things you learn to get over. Everyone makes mistakes.

A girl – late teens, blonde hair – had been standing at the bar with one foot crossed over the other, bent at the ankle. Long legs, black tights, short skirt, high cheekbones, a way looking round whenever the door swung open as if she was waiting for someone, or on the run. The ankles were the clue, or one of them. The red hair, the face almost white. This was on the evening of his first day's work at the new school, a day of lists and admin before the gates were opened wide, and Arnold had gone with two other teachers for a drink in town. Later, as the girl walked past the table where Arnold was sitting, she called back to the other girl and the older man she was drinking with: 'Make it a double,' she said, or 'Jan, mind my bag, will you?' The exact words didn't matter. Arnold knew exactly who she was, who she must be, though he'd never seen her in his life. When he next looked up he thought he'd missed his chance, but she was standing outside with the other girl, smoking. He tore a sheet off the timetable in his bag, wrote down his name and phone number, folded the paper and gave it to the girl, asking her to pass it on to her mother. She looked terrified. The older man came out to join them. He must have thought Arnold was trying his luck. As Arnold walked away he heard the laughter of her friends.

It would have happened anyway. It wasn't a big town. It was his home town, where he'd gone to school himself, though not at the place where he'd taken the job. Ellen, the girl's mother, had been his first love. Nothing and no one else would ever be needed – they had been going to get married.

Of course they were not going to get married. Her parents ran the Majestic, the town's second largest hotel; his parents were school teachers and they lived in the terraces behind the station. She was two years older. It was a phase, a whim, they were young. She was going to marry an airline pilot, or a lawyer.

~

The lawyer first, and a big wedding with a marquee on a hot July day in the grounds of the hotel and she wore a white dress with a veil, but she divorced him after just one year. He beat her with a hairbrush, the flat side that left no marks, usually, and to everything she accused him of he had a watertight defence, in the narrow eyes of the law. He covered his tracks. There followed a period of nothing but work, which consisted mostly of cleaning up after other people's fun. Then friends of her parents, who were also in the hotel business, came to visit with their son. They were already family, in a way. She married the son – a smaller affair this time, no need for the marquee or a band. She wore pale blue, with a yellow hat. She might have been one of the guests. Her parents gradually retired. Ellen and Mike took over the running of the hotel. He was full of grand schemes that left them heavily in debt. They sold the hotel to a chain and bought a sports hall, an old-fashioned place that smelt of stale sweat and that sharp, stinging lotion men rub into themselves so hard it looks like they're trying to rub themselves out, and two years later they had turned it into a fitness centre with exercise machines and aerobics classes and were again in debt.

'And Julie?' Arnold said.

'This was where she learned to ride a bike,' Ellen said. 'Over there.' She pointed towards a bandstand about fifty yards away.

She looked happy, remembering. They were sitting outside a café in the park that Arnold walked through daily to get to the school, with mugs of tea with the teabags still inside them. Did she also remember the night they had accidentally-on-purpose got themselves locked into this same park, a warm summer night, the grass prickly but dry beneath them, lying back under the stars, her skin so white, the red splay of her hair? It was brown now, and she had thickened and softened, and he hadn't recognised the woman walking fast down the path towards where he was already sitting until she had pulled out the chair – a movement that both rooted him to the spot and told him to vanish – and sat down opposite him.

'I meant, when did she come along?' Arnold said. He taught history, he'd made a vow to chronology.

'She didn't just walk up the street and knock on the door, you know.' Ellen was struggling to remember. 'She came along when we were still running the hotel. Not one of Mike's big ideas – this he *hadn't* planned – but the only one that lasted. We're a team, you know? Julie and me. Her father skipped off two years ago, went to South America.'

She paused, they both paused. 'Don't get any ideas, Mr Teacher Man.'

He didn't say, Are you happy? Is there someone else? She didn't say that there was. He said, 'What does she do?' Meaning Julie.

'What does she *do*?'

'I mean, what's she interested in? Does she go to the fitness centre?'

Ellen laughed. 'Never. She's cool, or whatever the word is. Hanging out at your mum's business is not that. She sees friends. She does her homework. She goes to the library after school, she gets it done, I don't have to keep on at her. She juggles.'

'She juggles what? Boyfriends?'

'School first. One thing, then the next. She spends hours in her room, doing the juggling, practising. She can do it with five balls but she wants more.'

'Of course she wants more. So she can stand in the park in the summer doing the juggling. It will bring her boys.'

'It'll bring her five-year-olds and dogs waiting for a ball to fall to the ground.'

Ellen rummaged in her bag and brought out a pack of cigarettes and lit one. She offered the packet and he shook his head. 'Everyone needs at least one vice,' she said.

He tried to think of one as simple as smoking, and failed. She asked him about his work, his life, why he'd left London, and he didn't want to talk about that but he did want to talk.

She was waiting.

Without even clearing his throat, he offered her a theory, warming to it as he continued because he wasn't getting much response but once started the thing did have to make its way. He might have been reciting lines from a play. He might have been applying for a job, the job he already had. His notion was this. Infancy: brute instinct, the Dark Ages, lit by flashes of inexplicable illumination. Childhood: the Middle Ages, the feudal system, know your place, rules about right and wrong. But adolescence, ah: hormones pumping, the body blossoming and the mind too, the birth of science, superstition in retreat, the voyages of exploration, the expansion of the world –

'You mean, Early Modern?'

'All that potential, for everything . . .' He hadn't known she knew the term, he wouldn't have guessed. 'It's the best age, the most exciting.'

'What about the Africans?' she said. 'What about the natives?'

Now he felt his age. The classrooms in the old days weren't even heated.

'And adulthood?'

'Modern, I guess.' He faced her, squaring up. 'Settling down, settling for form rather than content.'

'You mean, some good design? Better clothes, better shoes?'

He didn't know what he meant.

'Just faffing around? *Shopping?*'

She stood up, knocking over one of the mugs of tea. She walked away, or might as well have done. He'd touched something, a nerve, which hadn't been the intention but it was better than mild interest. He saw that she was different from who he'd imagined, remembered, pretended she was. Had he told her his theory before, his polished little speech? He couldn't have: a lifetime since he'd last seen her. But he knew that he sometimes repeated himself. Repetition – teaching the same matter, year after year, to a continuously renewing array of faces – was built in.

'We're just *shopping*?' she said again. She was doing it too. They stared at each other – one of them had to give, to laugh. This could become a pattern, until they established what each took to heart, and how lightly.

He righted the mug and mopped the table with paper tissues. 'Your word, not mine.'

It started spotting with rain. They should go inside.

'Is that still how they teach history?' she asked, forgiving. 'All those neat little periods?'

Yes, he supposed. It was what history was, one thing and then the next, as she'd said, with occasional changes of direction. How else would you do it? With hindsight, even revolutions were inevitable.

'It's more like being in a room with the walls closing in, and you have to find the way out before you get crushed,' she said. 'And you're blindfold.'

'And if you do get out in time?' he asked.

'You have to be lucky.'

'But if you do?'

'You're in another room. And the walls start doing that thing again.'

She laughed. She didn't mind the rain at all.

A jogger jogged by on the path in front of the café, his head moving faster than his legs to the beat of whatever was coming through his headphones. Then another, at a slightly faster pace: by the time they reached the tree near the gate, the second one would be in the lead. If they stayed a while longer they'd see their teenage selves walk by, his hand in her pants. Meanwhile, what appeared to be taking place, would certainly have appeared so to an eavesdropper at the next table, was an *appropriate* conversation between two friends who hadn't seen each other for a while – picking up loose threads, tying them neatly or agreeing to leave them loose. Was this what he'd left London for? Even if he'd known that she still lived here, he hadn't seriously imagined anything else; wishfully, perhaps, during nights when sleep wouldn't come, when he knew something had to be changed but not how, but he'd had no right to.

~

How, he had wondered as a child in the back of the car, watching the shops and the petrol stations and the fields and then more fields pass by, most of them empty of any animals, and the houses, endless, no distinction, random, and the weather so often grey, visibility poor, did the grown-ups know when to turn left, turn right, without checking the map? It came with the car. How did actors learn their lines? Hamlet had around one thousand five hundred. It came with the job. And with the names of the students he taught he could do this trick: within a day of taking over a new class he knew them all, not just of those who stuck up their hands and those who put out, made trouble, but the ones at the sides, heads down. It made a difference: he had their number, he'd got them taped, in their places.

They would have a name for him too by now, a made-up one, a word to be added to their textspeak, their tribal patois, which they input with their opposable thumbs on shiny tablets and sent through the sky. He wasn't curious, and nor in general were they. Early Modern, bodies and minds on the cusp, brimming with potential? – they slumped, most of them, and needed to be prodded or cajoled into showing any signs of active life. Their sleep patterns were awry, their minds elsewhere. Julie was among them, at the school, and though she wasn't in any of the classes he taught he was aware of her presence in the corridors, the communal spaces. She was aware of him, too. She was sixteen, seventeen, not as old as he'd guessed in the pub. Did Ellen know she drank in pubs with older men? It wasn't for Arnold to tell. Julie would see him and look away. Or, if he was busy with someone else, she wouldn't look away at all but pause and watch.

What had Ellen told her about himself? The truth, he supposed, or a version of it. He might once have become her father, except that if he had she wouldn't be who she was, herself, but another person entirely.

She had a tiny mouth, thin-lipped – that was the key difference, he decided, between Julie and Ellen. It was unlikely he'd learn more; something about her was withheld, though he didn't think she was shy. She spent long, patient hours, Ellen had said, practising her juggling with tennis balls in the attic bedroom she insisted on calling a boxroom, practising control to the point where it looked like carelessness – there was a thock, thock, from the ceiling above Ellen's own bedroom, and it was funny and then it was irritating. Sometimes, after a while, it was funny again. Surely that wasn't all she was doing in that room. Arnold wondered if he should be looking out for needle marks, cut marks, but he didn't want to call attention. There was a system in place, for referrals. 'In confidence,' it said, meaning anonymity, that no one would know who was doing the referring, but he failed to see how that could be so.

One morning, early, as he crossed the park on his way to the school, there was a figure on the bandstand. He remembered concerts in the summer, deckchairs, ice cream, its sticky sweetness. Now, the canopy and the railings rusted while the council debated endlessly whether to knock it

down or prop it up, but the figure he saw was perform-
ing: a girl, juggling. The sun hadn't broken through and
the air was damp, mist still clinging to the ground, and he
thought at first that this ghost in the mist was Ellen, Ellen
as she'd been, aged nineteen. It wasn't Ellen. It was Julie,
two years younger but they grew up faster these days. She
was varying the pace but at her quickest there was just a
flick of the wrists, and the balls she was tossing and catch-
ing, or whatever it was that she juggled, were invisible, like
the spokes of a wheel turning fast.

He wasn't alone: there were joggers, bicyclists, a woman
with three dogs, people on their way to work, like himself.
He couldn't understand why no one else stopped to watch.

The church at the junction near the school was now a
nightclub. The old swimming baths were an office block.
The whole town, once his entire world, was smaller; the
weather was more bland, less given to extremes, or perhaps
it was just he spent more time indoors and the heating was
better. He might have been watching a film he'd forgotten that he'd seen before: certain scenes familiar, déjà vu,
others he had no memory of, nor could he guess how they'd
end, what would happen next.

∾

The reception area was narrow and tight, presumably to
allow more space for the gym, with a door down a step that
led to the changing rooms. The girl at the desk knocked
on a second door he hadn't seen, behind her, and called a
name, and a big man who looked like he'd been left over
from when this building was a martial arts place came out
to show Arnold around. This was Gavin – Ellen had men-

tioned him, the manager. He wasn't so big that he filled the doorway. Behind him was Julie.

'Hello, Mr Hepworth.'

'Hello, Julie. Keeping fit?'

She was wearing some kind of gym kit. Her skin was shiny, she'd been working out. She smiled and closed the door.

The room with the exercise machines was low and dark and quiet, jittery with the flashing light of music videos on a wide screen with the sound turned low. Just three or four indeterminate bodies were moving rhythmically on the exercise machines. Somewhere masculine, like a munitions factory or a place of punishment. Coming out, Arnold touched grease on the door handle. Maybe the whole operation was a front for something else. He asked if there was a pool and Gavin said yes, of course there was a pool, but it was closed just now, a problem with the filtration. Maybe next week.

Of course, for a teacher – there was a dig here, teachers being people who needed to be thrifty, peripheral to mainline capitalism – there'd be a discount on the membership fee . . . No, Arnold said, not now, he'd think about it. They were back at reception, and the girl at the desk needed to show Gavin a printout. The other door opened, the door behind, and Julie was looking out at Arnold. She mouthed something, and he went closer, and then she'd taken his hand in hers and they were inside the room and she'd closed the door.

A desk, a leather sofa, a wash basin with paper towels, one of those medical examination beds which the doctor tells you to lie on while he fusses with some lightweight inspection tool. A large photograph of a football team, scribbled with felt-tip signatures. The heating was up so high it felt like a sauna.

'Don't tell, will you?'

He heard 'Talk to me', but knew that couldn't be right. 'About what?' he said.

She rolled her eyes. She was dealing with a deliberately obtuse child. Her hand was still around his wrist. 'That you saw me here, this afternoon. You're not going to tell her, are you?'

Her being Ellen. That was the easy bit.

'It's not what you think,' the girl said.

They could hear Gavin's voice outside, impatient. He didn't know what he thought, but he was beginning to. She didn't go to the library after school to do her homework, or maybe some days she did but not all. Gavin was muscle but he had manners too, some charm, some cunning.

'I'm not here,' she said. 'Simple as that. You don't know me.' She put a finger, vertical, across her tiny lips. She was going to lick it, it occurred to him, so he helped her along: he took her wrist, licked her finger, placed it over his own mouth. She grinned, as if they'd found a common language.

∼

He phoned Ellen and asked her to lunch and she said yes, where was he thinking of going, and he said, jokingly, the Majestic, which hadn't been the Majestic for a long time but they went there anyway. They were archaeologists, they would dig down and reclaim it. It was beyond reclamation: walls had been knocked down, corridors had vanished, every new shade of grey and beige and placid purple had been chosen from an online chart by a remote buyer in head office. She shrugged. At least no one here knew who she was.

The food was without pretensions and unexpectedly good. They were Class of '81, just the two of them, the two who had bothered to turn up, and Ellen filled in the others. Two had cancer, five were divorced, four of those remarried. Keith, the star athlete whose records still stood, was serving behind the counter in a post office. Susan – Arnold couldn't remember her, which was the whole point of the story – was living with a film producer in Hollywood, a woman, and ran a fashion business in LA.

'People can change,' he said.

'Yes, if they want to. Most people don't get around to it, they're too busy.'

And the teachers: she had gone to the retirement party of Mr Hoskins, and he'd got drunk and asked how many of the teachers present had slept with another member of staff. Someone had put up their hand and asked if supply teachers counted. There was a discussion about this, and a vote was taken. Like at the General Synod, he said. She couldn't recall the result. About most of the other teachers, between the quick and the dead, who was still alive and who not, they had no way of knowing.

They came back for an early weekday supper, and then they came again. They were through with school. The dining room – never busy, but not so empty that words bounced back off the walls – was a comfortable place to be. The old hotel with its uncarpeted back stairs and potted palms in big brass pots had been taken away and they'd been given this one in exchange, but weren't in a position to complain. They were becoming regulars: soon the waiter, clumsy but with a degree in hospitality, would be asking, 'The usual, madam?'

Arnold – 'May I?' – took a forkful of Ellen's risotto. 'Did your parents – ?'

'Did they know we were fucking? They had other things to worry about. The chef who called in sick. The rat droppings in the store room. The underage drinking –'

'Did we do that too?'

'Where did all that vodka go that didn't go through the till? They never thought. Thank god I got out of that. Hotels are twenty-four hours, non-stop.'

'Or they did know, but didn't want to know?'

Her parents – Arnold remembered the anxious, hurrying father, the mother tall and dressing each day for a party she was always about to go to – had been polite to him, even kind. But they *must* have known. How could he and their daughter be doing what they did and it be a secret? It must have been obvious to the whole world.

'I don't think even that.'

'Why *didn't* we get married?'

She shook her head. Her competence, her independence, placed her beyond his reach, except for the time in the park when he had unwittingly made her angry. Ordering a second bottle of wine, Arnold suggested they move in. Or at least take a room, a suite, for the afternoon.

'We don't have to do anything. We could just lie there and watch TV.'

'We could read all those books we never have time to.'

'We could trash it, like rock stars.'

He has passed these rooms, the door ajar: inside, two chambermaids are bundling sheets, spraying and wiping the surfaces, talking in some Eastern European language as they work. Or there's a damp towel thrown across the bed, or a hand is reaching awkwardly to cut toenails. The window slides open only three inches before it hits a stop, in case you've come here to throw yourself out. No action here has consequences. At some time that afternoon, in the carelessness that comes with having nothing to be guarded against, he mentioned the anonymous notes that had been posted in his internal mail at the school, the obscene notes that he was planning to ignore, and Ellen laughed, and at another point he spilled the beans, mentioned that he'd seen Julie at the fitness centre.

~

She came to him in a break between lessons. Children and other teachers were milling around, laughter and clatter, things spilling onto the floor, a bell clanging. There was never any time; everything took place at once. She was pushing a sheet of paper towards him. She had a doctor's appointment and to get there she needed to leave school now, twenty minutes ago, and someone had to sign the form so they'd let her out at the gate and she couldn't find her year leader. She needed permission. He signed.

~

There was a blow-up, of a kind that would need a public inquiry to unravel. Ellen, having discovered *financial irregularities*, went to the fitness centre and sacked Gavin on the spot. Julie hadn't come home. She was found on a roadside verge five miles out of town, semi-conscious but sitting up, by a passing driver at 3 a.m. She had been thrown from the car that was smashed against a dry-stone wall, with Gavin still inside it. The passing driver, who had been drinking and didn't want the police, called his wife, who had once trained as a nurse and who woke up her neighbour, who happened to be a retired policeman, and they drove out in his car.

Julie had concussion, no more. Someone used the word 'miracle'. Someone wrote to the local paper pointing out that if she had been wearing a seat belt she'd be dead. Gavin had broken forty-nine bones.

A month later, after Arnold had handed in his notice and then changed his mind and asked if he could retract it, and had been told they'd be more than pleased for him to stay, Ellen phoned to say she was taking Julie to the airport and would he drive them. Her father in Brazil had invited her over for as long as she needed, as long as she wanted. Julie was thrilled; already she was changed, relaxed, her movements softer and less guarded. Arnold remembered a boy at a previous school where he'd worked, a severely dyslexic boy who after falling from a first-floor balcony had suddenly become able to read and write with perfect fluency. Now she talked easily, as an equal, about how she planned to catch up on the school work she might be missing, and she didn't object to Arnold coming to the airport. He had been rendered harmless, thinking in his teachery, dufferish way as he balanced a tray of coffees in the departure lounge, having got there with time to spare: what she'll find in the new country will be different from what she thinks to find, and different from what anyone can tell her. There will be spices, promises, massacres, shopping malls, betrayals, loneliness, happiness. Speakeasies – he has never been in a speakeasy, he hardly knows what one is. There will be a hawk circling at dawn, of course, but there'll also be insects that bite and that get into your clothes in the night. There'll be species that haven't even been named. Not that the names matter; the species have been around for millennia without them.

Her luggage was carry-on, under the limit, what more could she need, whisked through.

By that time, well into the new year, he had moved out of the house he'd been sharing with another teacher and was living in a flat on a new-build scheme for key workers. He was going out with Ginny, first-year teacher, Geography. Two days a week after school they went jogging, through the park, past the bandstand, along the canal, up the hill, rain or shine, and she stayed over. She was worried she hadn't done the right thing, she had never really wanted to be a teacher. What, then? And what was wrong with teaching? She looked at him as if she couldn't believe that he'd just asked that question, then giggled and turned away. Her legs, the touch of her skin, were wonders of the world. He said that some people are just late developers and that was okay, if they got there in the end. He himself, for example, had never really known what love was until he had found her, Ginny, and it had taken him some time, and two marriages, to get here. He didn't hurry to tell her this; it would sound pre-arranged, it would be tempting fate. But then he did, of course. And she was happy, but he could sense a holding back, a reluctance to believe that anyone really meant what they said, especially if they said it in bed, or with bed in mind. Superstitions were involved.

She falls asleep with her fingers over her lips, like a child, not to let out what she might speak in the night. He imagines that, if he were to go into Julie's room and pick up the padded balls from wherever she's left them and start to toss them, to trust them to the air and his hands to receive them, he'll find himself juggling like a professional, without a single spill, with no one to see, in that room that isn't his.

WHITE DOGS

White dog one: lying, occasionally scratching, in the shade beneath the canopied roof of the station.

Emmeline Davitsky stepped over the dog. She was big-boned, strong, independent, with a helmet of frizzy bronze hair, and she had no need for a porter to carry her bags. Strangers gave her right of way. She also had a delicate touch: with a fine-haired sable brush, she could paint every leaf on a tree, every hair on a dog. She was in demand. In her high-ceilinged studio in a London street lined with trees that blossomed pink in the spring, she painted hyper-realistic portraits of the pampered pets of the rich, though she rarely got to see these animals at first hand – her clients sent her photographs, large cheques and the required dimensions. It was time she got out into the real world, she had decided; it was time for fresh air, time for some flesh and blood.

A hot July afternoon. The train moved on towards the coast; two teenage boys on the platform, the only witnesses to Emmeline's arrival, returned to their task of prising open the cash box of the refreshments dispenser with a blunt penknife. A lime-green car with a dent in its front fender drew up and the driver leaned across to open the passenger door.

'Miss Davitsky?'

Emmeline approached the car.

'I'm Frank,' the driver said, and he plucked from the dashboard a card for ABC Radio Taxis. 'The Castle Guest House won't set you back too much,' he said. 'And Ella does a grand breakfast. Black pudding to die for. Are you vegetarian?'

'I didn't know there was a castle,' Emmeline replied.

'There isn't,' Frank said. 'But it's not a bad name for a bed-and-breakfast.'

He was white-haired and red-faced and stood no higher than Emmeline's shoulders. 'I see you've brought your equipment,' he said, opening the boot for her luggage. Meanwhile, white dog one ambled towards the car with its tail wagging, and after he had stacked Emmeline's cases in the boot Frank patted the dog behind its ears and gave it a mint from a packet he kept in the front.

Emmeline had to move a newspaper, two empty crisp bags and a mangled Coke tin from the back seat before she got in. And there was an odd smell: a dog smell, she decided, noticing the hairs on the rug she was sitting on. A dog smell mingled with a Frank smell. It would be hard to disentangle them.

They drove off. 'This is a quiet place,' Frank offered. 'Not much to write home about.'

What had she expected? She was in the sticks, it was crazy to have ever left town, she was going to be kidnapped and ritually disembowelled by satanists.

White dog two: cocking its leg against the base of a lamp post while they waited for the traffic lights to change. Coincidence. Though Emmeline did pay attention to that clean white hair, a single all-over colour; a mottled dog was by comparison a simple job.

White dog three: padding along the pavement with a

newspaper clamped in its mouth, straight out of the 1950s. Rufus, she thought, remembering a dog she had once known. But this dog was different.

'These white dogs . . .' Emmeline began.

'There was some folk down from the university the other week,' Frank said. 'They were staying with Ella too, while they did their testing.'

'What were they testing?'

'The dogs, of course.'

These dogs, Frank explained, were ferociously intelligent. They listened to what you said, and you felt that if they could talk back they'd have something to contribute that might change your mind. And if Emmeline wasn't in a hurry and would be happy to reach the Castle Guest House via the scenic route, Frank would explain how they came about.

She met his eyes in the rear-view mirror – she had never seen such jutting eyebrows – and nodded.

About four years before, the editor of the local newspaper had received a letter on the subject of animal rights. A hundred years from now, the writer claimed, people would look back on the barbaric ways in which we now treated animals with same abhorrence as we now look on slavery, or child labour. (Emmeline yawned; a private thing, more like a burp, as her head was already bent and she didn't have room to stretch.) It was a well-written letter, but the editor didn't print it. The letters page was a forum to discuss where the new town refuse dump should be sited, or what to do about underage drinking at the weekends; it wasn't the right place to start changing the world. (But where *is* the right place? Emmeline wondered. She was not unhappy with the world as it was.) Besides, one of the directors of the company that owned the newspaper happened also to own a large poultry farm where the hens were kept in battery cages, and which provided employment for a number of local people.

For the same reasons, the next three letters from the same correspondent were also not printed.

'Noam Chomsky?' said Frank. He seemed to be looking at a particular house built from the local stone and set back from the road.

'Noam Chomsky lives here?' said Emmeline.

'He has to live *somewhere*.' Frank laughed. 'I mean, you're familiar with his work?'

She said yes, then added that she wasn't *very* familiar, it was a long time since she'd read him.

The first letter, Frank explained, had suggested that Noam Chomsky's theory of a universal grammar, innate to humans, might also be relevant to other species, whose communicative abilities were far more sophisticated than generally understood. The second letter returned to the subject of animal rights, and included an attack on the practices of the local battery farm as well as a six-page appendix of statistics. The third letter Frank had no idea about, but he thought it was probably along the same lines.

The editor left the appendix to the second letter unread, but he was intrigued enough to invite Arthur J. Park to come in to the newspaper's office. He sensed a story here, a profile of a local eccentric, and even if not he could suggest to the correspondent a more appropriate journal for his ideas.

'This editor,' Emmeline wondered aloud.

'A young chap,' Frank said. 'But he's settling in.'

'And this Mr Park – he's a local man?'

'Been in the area for years,' Frank said. 'Do you want to

see the church while we're here? This is the Baptists, the C of E's in the main street.'

Four teenagers were sitting on the wall by the gate to the church, sharing a bottle of cider. As the car slowed Emmeline thought she should get out – it was the country air she had come for, after all – but four against one was not good odds. She told Frank to carry on with his story.

Arthur J. Park wrote back to the editor, suggesting lunch at his home. So the editor called Frank and, following Park's detailed instructions, they drove out to a converted farmhouse on the outskirts of the town. A maid opened the door and led the editor through the house to a table laid for two in the garden, where a woman and a dog were waiting.

The woman was small, with hair almost pure white, and somehow familiar. (Witchcraft, Emmeline thought, and she was not far wrong.) In her early fifties, the editor guessed, though it was difficult to tell because she clearly took pains to look younger than whatever her real age must be. She introduced herself as Elizabeth Lovelli and paused, waiting for a response. And indeed the editor, taking a moment to reflect, did recognise the name. Back in the early 1970s Elizabeth Lovelli had been a presenter on a children's TV programme, all sweetness and honey spiced with a calculated amount of cheek, just ripe for a scandal, and then it came, on cue – drugs, sex, it was so long ago it could have been just a four-letter word – and Lovelli had disappeared to America. Silence for a few years – a view, just then, as the car turned a corner and the ground fell away to the left, of a new housing estate pasted over the farmland, not yet weathered in, and Emmeline shivered – but then she had reappeared as an actress in a number of films by a famous European director. There'd been a feminist element: she had played women who refused to conform, being unafraid to bare to the camera a body that was no longer young.

While the editor struggled to remember the titles of the films, Elizabeth Lovelli introduced the dog, a white bull terrier – who was Arthur J. Park, the author of the letters.

'You mean,' said Emmeline, 'that dog knew how to use a computer?'

Frank laughed again, a loud guffaw that included spittle. Emmeline was glad she was sitting in the back seat.

'Of course not,' said Frank. 'How could any dog use its paws to operate a keyboard?'

Lovelli herself had typed the letters, he explained, as a secretary would, and had helped with some of the research, but every word in them had been dictated to her by the dog.

An eccentric, thought the editor, and worth at least a half-page story with a photo of the bull terrier: *A Dog Writes* ... But he was a fair man, and as lunch progressed – roasted vegetables, home-baked bread, apple tart – he decided that this woman deserved better. She was rational and charming and had persuasive eyes. Clearly, dogs can communicate emotions, so why not, if you know how to listen to them, ideas too? They can remember things, so why not imagine them? They are intelligent, and have a down-to-earth, grass-roots perspective on human behaviour; they don't have to worry about interest rates or job security or losing votes. They don't have votes to lose. They'd need glasses to read newspapers but they can hear between every spoken word and can smell hypocrisy at a hundred paces. And because their days are not filled with shopping and paying bills and picking up the car from the garage and planning trips to Hawaii, they have time, enough time to become true scholars.

Park ambled towards the newspaper editor and sniffed his outstretched hand, then turned to Lovelli. There was a warning in that sniff. More constant than any husband (and she'd had at least three, Frank believed), Park would remain loyal to his mistress until death. For the rest of the lunch he lay by the table in the shade with one forepaw stretched in front of him and the other tucked under his short neck; his head was tilted to one side and his eyes were closed.

Another letter from Park arrived on the editor's desk. This was not expected: both the dog and Elizabeth Lovelli must have known that it wouldn't be printed. It was about the rarity of genuine communication, even between members of the same species, and went on to recommend that the editor take up yoga to counteract the stress of his work. At the end of the letter was a handwritten note from Lovelli herself, telling the editor that Arthur J. Park had really taken to him. The editor replied, informally: *Dear Arthur . . .*

Two more times Frank drove the editor out to the farmhouse, where he sat down to lunch with the former actress and the dog. Having ruled out a dog story, he was hoping to coax from Lovelli tales of Hollywood from the inside: gossip, anecdotes, meetings with the greats. She was, besides, a striking woman; it wasn't just her eyes that told of why the camera had loved her; and though professional interests suggested that on at least one visit he should have taken the newspaper's photographer with him, he chose not to. But while she remained eager to talk, she insisted on discussing animal rights, linguistics and the internal contradictions of capitalism. When the editor tried to steer the conversation towards her films, Arthur J. Park made a low warning growl.

And then, a month after the final lunch, when the editor had almost given up on both the woman and the dog, he got his story. The phone was ringing as he entered his office: Lovelli, gulping back her sobs, told him that Park had been kidnapped.

At the farmhouse, Frank, the editor and Lovelli stared in silence at the splintered frame of the French windows and the trampled rose-beds, while a maid swept up the broken glass. Then Lovelli took them to her study and showed them the ransom note she had found pinned to the wall. The note declared that Elizabeth Lovelli would get her dog back only if she agreed to provide funding for a film of *The Lady with the Dog*, and herself play the part of Anna Sergeyevna.

The script, an adaptation of Chekhov's short story, was written by the kidnapper herself, Felicia Green, a mature film student who had been hanging around film studios in Los Angeles and London for a decade, trying to get backers for her project. Constant rejection had made her only more determined. This was her final, desperate bid, and she couldn't allow herself to fail. A week after the kidnapping Lovelli received in the post a package containing Arthur J. Park's tail, neatly cut off at the base.

Prompted and supported by the editor, Elizabeth Lovelli renewed her contacts with the film world, called in favours owed and took out all her savings. It took around three months, during which she sent anguished messages to the kidnapper concerning the proper care of Arthur J. Park – to endure hot sunshine, his short-haired body needed continual bathing with protective lotion – and pleading for the deadline to be extended. But finally the money was in place, the director and actors contracted, and the film went into production.

The result was a curiosity. The script was banal and full of anachronisms. The casting of the two main characters managed to reverse the ages and experience of the originals – Gurov in the story is described as being almost twice Anna's age; in the film, Lovelli in her fifties played against a twenty-four-year-old stage actor eager to make his break into movies. In Felicia Green's script, both Anna's husband and Gurov's wife were completely unsympathetic characters, which made the love affair between Anna and Gurov predictable and unsurprising. Only in its main narrative episodes and certain incidental details did the film remain faithful to Chekhov's story – Anna's white Pomeranian lapdog, for example, was exactly that, a fox-faced bundle of fur.

The driver of the carriage in which the lovers ride out of town was played by Frank. He had only two lines to speak, but he took his whip home to practise with and soon he could use it to lightly flick the rumps of his horses. He still had the whip; he kept it in the boot of the car, if Emmeline would like to see it?

She demurred.

White dog four: excreting on a wide patch of verge, straining to get the job done, while its owner read his book on a nearby bench. To Emmeline, the dog's awkward, rigid pose suggested heraldry; the word 'rampant' came to mind.

Certain scenes in the final cut appeared rushed, impatient. This was despite Felicia Green's wearisome attempts to slow everything down – for example, in the scene when, after Anna and Gurov first make love, Gurov cuts himself a slice of watermelon and there follows, according to

Chekhov, at least half an hour of silence as he ponders her statement that he will now despise her. The haste was due to the discovery, halfway through filming, that the white Pomeranian had been made pregnant by Arthur J. Park. On the day that the final scenes were completed it gave birth to four mongrel but pure white puppies.

SOMEWHERE AT SIX

For lunch the boy asks for scrambled eggs, but they had scrambled eggs for breakfast. No, he says, they had cake. What kind of cake? He thinks about this. Monkey cake, he says. They stare at each other, which he enjoys: it is a test to see who will blink first. He is seven years old. His face is wide and tanned and serious beneath a shock of hair blacker than night. He is a child who was born in Chile and then shipped in, adopted, translated. C blinks. He is adamant, a king by divine right and not to be crossed, and she will play chief minister, catering – literally – to his every whim.

They walk to the shop around the corner to buy more eggs. This is not a battle worth fighting: it is not actually illegal to have scrambled eggs for both breakfast and lunch, and for supper too if he wants. C has known men who start drinking alcohol at midday, earlier, and continue until the small hours and she never tried to stop them; although it's possible that that is what they, some of them, were hoping she might do. The boy, too old to hold her hand, walks in front, asserting his independence, his maleness; but if anything befalls him, this precious, uninsured cargo in her charge, he knows he has back-up.

While they are eating the eggs Hannah phones, the boy's mother. After several years in Budapest Hannah has come back to London, bringing her adopted son but leaving behind her Hungarian husband. C has known Hannah since schooldays: Hannah is a woman who packs efficiently, who enjoys making decisions about what must come with her and what can be let go, who enjoys this so much that she has made of her life a series of situations in which these decisions cry out to be made. This weekend she is in Brighton with a man she met a month ago at work, a client, an old-school wine merchant in search of a marketing strategy. C is staying with the child in Hannah's south London flat; caretaking is what friends are for.

Everything is fine, she tells Hannah. She doesn't mention that the boy didn't fall asleep last night until after midnight, nor that he wet the bed, nor that the washer-dryer in the kitchen has given up on drying, so the sheets are still wet. Enjoy, she tells Hannah. Does she want to speak to her son?

The boy takes another mouthful of egg and chews solemnly before he comes to the phone. Yes, he says. No. Perhaps. He says that they had scrambled eggs for both breakfast and lunch. 'When are you coming home?'

The morning's cloud cover has dispersed, the sun is out and is warm, they will go to the park. But first, C goes downstairs and knocks on the door of the ground-floor flat, introduces herself, and asks if she can hang the wet sheets on the washing line she has seen in the garden at the back. The launderette might have been simpler, except for needing a pocketful of small change, or asking for Hannah's advice on the phone, but she didn't, and now C is talking to a tall man who is both nervous – he keeps glancing behind him – and over-friendly. He has a stammer. He leans close. He seems to have difficulty understanding what she wants – possibly no one has made this request ever before – but soon they are side by side in the garden, hanging the sheets on the washing line. He says she is welcome, he hardly uses the line, he doesn't do much washing.

Does the boy need sun cream? Where would Hannah keep this? She has seen a sun hat in the boy's bedroom and suggests that he wear it. The boy agrees, but only on condition that she wear a hat too, and because she thinks it might be natural at his age – she cannot remember – to believe that life is fair, she goes along with this. He says that Hannah has a sun hat but they cannot find it. The only hat they come across is a builder's hard hat, bright yellow, on the table in Hannah's bedroom – now C's, for two nights, one of which has been survived. Unexpectedly, the hat fits. Does it belong to the man Hannah is now with in Brighton? It's hardly the hat of a wine merchant. It suggests something rougher, more hard-core.

Her phone rings. 'Darling, are you well? How's the boy? Have you packed him off to boot camp?'

It is James, her husband, calling from the country. She stopped living with him three months ago, she lives in London now, but he still calls her almost every day and speaks to her as if she'll be home in time for supper.

'There's been a power cut,' he says – well, not everything, just certain rooms, but the microwave is off, everything in the kitchen, he thinks it's just a fuse but where is the fuse box? And does he just flip a switch?

C reminds him that he has lived in that house for twenty years. More, he corrects her. Nearer thirty.

There is a message on her phone that must have arrived while she was hanging out the sheets. From M – he has been to her flat, which is really James's flat but is now hers, if occupiers have rights, and where is she? She calls him back and laughs when he picks up, his voice so serious.

She explains, tells him the name of the park where she'll be for the next two hours, and becomes aware that the boy is watching her.

'Who was that?' the boy asks.

A friend.

They leave, but not before the boy has gone to fetch his own mobile phone, because if she has hers he needs his too. It's a new phone, an expensive one, too expensive for a seven-year-old, but all the other children have these things, Hannah has told her.

'You don't need your phone today,' C says.

'What if I get lost?' he argues.

She shakes her head.

'What if *you* get lost? How will you tell me if I don't have my phone?'

She gives in. She puts two apples in her handbag. She asks the boy if he wants to go for a pee before they leave – she has seen him doing this, seen him shaking his willy so vigorously to disperse the last drops that Hannah must have taught him this, it can't be how all boys do it, or must signify some deep private anxiety. He says no. She puts on the yellow hard hat and shoulders the boy's three-wheeled scooter – not heavy, but an awkward L-shape. So much of childcare is manual labour.

~

C and the boy are eating ice creams at a table outside the café in the park. They are not the only ones. The park is thronged with Saturday-afternoon picnickers and strollers and frisbee-throwers; the litter bins are overflowing. In the playground adjacent to the café a veiled woman is bent over a buggy saying cootchy-coo. Another woman is pushing a girl on a swing, bowing like d'Artagnan or Sir Walter Raleigh or that flunkey in *Hamlet*, what was his name, Osric?, when the swing sails away, then standing to receive the laughing girl on her return and give another push. *Again, again* – the woman will tire of this sooner than the child but she'll go on for as long as there is laughter. Until she stops nothing else need happen.

After finishing his ice cream the boy hunches over his phone, his thumbs peevishly swiping its screen, sending apes, pigs, whole civilisations to kingdom come. He is trigger-happy. They might as well have stayed at home. He is too old for the swings and see-saw in the playground, but leaning against the table is the three-wheeled scooter.

'Why don't you go for a ride?' C says.

The boy looks surprised. She might be suggesting he fly to the moon. Just around the park, she says. Maybe over to where they play basketball, and the paddling pool. About ten minutes, say?

As soon as he has gone she feels not relief but as if she has been abandoned. He has left his sun hat behind – a promise that he'll return, but she knows that he knows that promises are just things you make to see how far they'll stretch, and she suspects he knows she knows this. So now she has nothing to do except what a woman sitting alone is assumed to be doing, which is waiting, which makes her feel vulnerable – to looks, stares, other people's stories.

She picks up a newspaper travel supplement that someone has left on the bench beside her: boutique hotels in Bratislava, rough riding in the Outer Hebrides. She calls M. He says he is on his way but the Northern line is closed, he'll have to find a bus.

'Are you free tonight?' he asks.

She reminds him that she is looking after a child, and that children can't just be turned off when not convenient.

The briefest of pauses, then he says that he'll cook something for all of them.

'Is there anything I should buy?' she asks. 'Eggs?'

'No, I'll bring everything. The kid isn't vegetarian, is he?'

He has children of his own, a girl and a boy. She has never met them but knows all of their abilities and their limits, even some of their jokes. At first, talking about them, he was shy, but when she positioned herself to listen he talked, he wanted to. He just needed permission. It is a form of infidelity, another one, in which he luxuriates.

A pigeon is puttering on the table, pecking at the crumbs of ice-cream cone. C wants to shoo it off but a child, yet another one, has come to stand by the table and is talking to it in pigeon language.

She looks at her watch and sees that more than twenty minutes have passed since the boy went off on his scooter. She calls the boy's number, but his phone appears to be dead. Half an hour. She can't go to look for him because what if he comes back while she has gone and finds she isn't there? The yellow and pink flowers in the circular bed are so bright they hurt her eyes. She will tell someone, ask them to keep an eye open while she's away. She hears a scream, a shriek – turns, and sees a small child being held upside down by her father, who then swings the child by its legs around in a circle. Still screaming, the child is delirious with joy. She looks away and thinks she sees M approaching the café, his determined walk, as if always he has to catch up, with what he has no idea, but then she sees that it isn't M, that she's been tricked by some random affinity – gait, height, shape and turn of the head.

She calls James but then cancels and calls M again but

before he can pick up there he is, the boy, at the gate to the café, crying, clinging on to his scooter. He is shepherded towards her by a matronly woman who has already decided so finally that C is careless, selfish and plain stupid that there's no point in even pretending she is not.

She could claim that she is not the boy's mother, which would make her even worse.

His phone has been stolen by two bigger boys, who ambushed him on their bikes and then sped away.

She kneels and wraps the boy in her arms, expecting resistance but it does not come, and she is almost grateful then to the thieves because there is a chance that between her and the boy things are going to be easier now. When boy's sobbing subsides and his breathing has become more regular, she calls the police – for an insurance claim they will need a number, a reference. Getting through to the right person involves much repetition of information, like shopping online, but she knows she is doing the right thing.

Astoundingly, a police car arrives at the park gate within minutes. As if it had been parked around the corner, waiting. The two policeman – one white, one black – are like solemn schoolboys: they listen, nodding, and C knows she could be telling them anything, that the phone has been stolen by aliens or that the boy is the king of Siam or that she has been raped in broad daylight, in front of this whole crowd of people, and they would just carry on nodding. This is, she understands, supposed to be *reassuring*. The nod – the timing, the angle – has been a part of their training. Years ago, decades, during prayers at primary school she was taught to nod her head whenever the name Jesus was mentioned and it was never a natural thing, either she listened to what the prayer was saying and forgot all about

Jesus or she kept her ears open for just that one word, and even then she got the timing wrong. Then the policemen tell C and the boy to get into the back of their car, and somehow the scooter is fitted in too and the two hats, the sun hat and the yellow plastic helmet, and the one next to the driver turns round in his seat and tells the boy to keep his eyes peeled because they are going to drive around the nearby streets looking for the boys who have stolen the phone.

No one is going to stand on the street corner waiting for them, waving the phone, waving a white flag, saying *me, me*, take me to your cells and beat me up. This is pointless, and the boy knows it better than any of them: he is fiddling with the button that winds the window up and down, not looking out at all. After the third circuit of the same streets they drive to the police station.

As they get out of the car C asks if she can make a phone call. The policemen look at her as if she's asked if she can hang her sheets on their washing line. Then the eyes of the black one drift away, he is losing interest. The white one is overweight, not much but he's sweating, has probably been sweating all day in his padded jacket and all-seasons trousers and his wife or girlfriend or mother does a daily wash, the ironing too. They are blunt instruments. They are young, of course, she doesn't hold that against them. It's more that their apparatus, their buckles and clips, their too many pockets, makes them boxy, awkward, the opposite of streamlined. It's all padding. They might be good in a terrorist attack but faced with the everyday messiness of the world, let alone the job of policing it, their gruffness and air of command must surely be a front, no less than the criminal's put-on innocence (*Who? Me?*).

She calls Hannah but Hannah's phone is switched off – if

you go away with a man for a weekend, even to the seaside, you probably do spend most of the time in bed. And M, where is M? She calls him.

'I'm on my way,' he says. 'The traffic – I'll be there in twenty minutes.'

She explains that she is not now in the park but at the police station. Except for sometimes, very late, too late for the normal etiquette to apply, he is never good on the phone. He blusters a joke: does she need someone to stand bail, a character reference? 'Good in bed' – it would be a waste of the world's finite resources to lock her away. His timing is poor, his timing is terrible – why wasn't he with her in the park, when she needed him?

'Please come,' she says.

He says he'll try but he has to be somewhere at six, he's not now sure if he can make it –

'Where?' she says.

'Where what?'

'Where do you have to be at six?'

Never, until now, in all the time she has known him, has she ever worried about him seeing other women. They have joked about it; she has even pointed out to him women in the street who might interest him, younger ones, obvious ones. What happened to the meal that he said he would cook for them?

'I'll call later,' M says.

The boy is looking at her, as are the two policemen. Haven't they got football to talk about, to pass the time, or serial killers?

Then they are inside the police station, and then they are sitting at a table in a room on the first floor with a policewoman who wants the boy to look at some photographs. She is like a friendly librarian; if she wasn't in fact a policewoman, you might trust her with your secrets, or at least swap recipes. She has three thick folders; she opens the first in front of the boy and begins slowly to turn the pages. Each page shows the faces of twelve men. Young men, without fear, and known to the police. They are infinite. The boy is interested at first, it is a game, and the policewoman too, hoping for a spark of recognition – a response, eager, even if only to something as slight and in passing as C was deceived by in the park, when she thought she saw M approaching. She is waiting for the boy's eyes to widen and his finger to point . . . This one? This one with earrings? This shy one? This one who is pulling a face? This one with scars on both of his cheeks, almost but not quite symmetrical, as if the person making them has slipped? It is like looking through the files of a dating agency. This one with broken teeth? This one with no eyebrows? This one in whose mouth butter would not melt? This one whose ears stick out at right angles? One of them, surely; if not on this page, then the next. They are spoilt for choice. These men have nothing in common except that each has brushed, if only lightly, against the law, has stepped out of line.

At a point early in the second folder the child is becoming bored and is slumping in his chair. C also. The light has changed: outside, she notices, the sunshine has yielded to clouds, and rain is falling. The sheets hanging in the garden will be getting wet, unless the nervous man has thought to bring them in. He is tall, he will barely need to reach up to unpeg them. He will be hopeless at folding them, by himself, but he will gather the pegs carefully, in a plastic bag, and put them in a drawer. But when she looks back to the table and sees that the policewoman too is starting to give up, knowing that the boy's attention span is limited, and is turning the pages more quickly, she wants to tell her to slow down. It's not fair – she can play this game too – that the ones in folders two and three should receive more cursory attention. The one with half-closed eyes. The one who has just tasted something sour. The one who is sixty if he's a day. The one with a tattoo of a rope around his neck. The one who is chewing. The one who is terrified. The one with broken teeth *and* a broken nose. The one who is laughing, proud to have been included, or dismissive. The one who is wearing a bobble hat / reversed baseball cap / bandanna / woman's scarf. The one who is about to break into tears. The one who is upside down. The one who looks as if he's eleven years old. The one who looks no less bored than the child. The one who could be a girl – and where *are* the girls, C wants to ask, there must be a separate folder, girls make mistakes too, girls know how to fuck up their lives just as much as boys, but for now she'll make do with what's here, with what's on offer. The one who is surely the twin brother of the one at the top of the previous page. The one who is so out of focus he could be anyone. The one who looks like M must have looked twenty years ago, half his life, when he was at college. The one who appears to be asleep. The one whose face is burnt, the burning man, victim of a roadside bomb. The one who is wearing lipstick. The one with eyes so pale he could be blind. The one who is looking into the middle distance, beyond her. C opens her bag and offers an apple to the boy, who refuses it, so she offers it to the policewoman instead. The one she has met, she could swear it, at a party only last month. The one who can't see out. The one who is sweating, who has been running all his life. She bites into the apple, and places the second apple on the table beside the yellow hard hat. It is like a still life, for the wall of a provincial museum. The room is warm and grey. A calmness has settled on her, inside her. She rests her hand on the boy's shoulder and he looks at her with misplaced trust, asking to go home. Not yet. Can they go back to the start, re-wind, look again, knowing what she knows now, which is something if not much? It's not as if they're in a hurry. She is here for the duration.

TIREDNESS CAN KILL

He doesn't want to know about *markets in turmoil*. But after picking up the free newspaper from the seat across the aisle and putting on his reading glasses he glances at the opening paragraphs and soon he is feeling the reckless glee he has known when his team is not just losing but losing without any hope of making a game of it, they are not even *trying*, they are not even pretending that his support means or has ever meant anything at all to them and he wants them to lose with abandon, with a scoreline so hilarious as to be historic.

He knew, the moment he saw the sculptor's photograph in the catalogue, that this was the man Alicia had left him for. He looked closely at the sculptor's face, and then he looked at the heavy sheets of metal, folded and bent and precariously balanced on the polished wood floor, and at the way the metal sheets were joined together, welded or with bolted plates. The photograph was not of a man who welded. The welding had been left to assistants, charged with translating the master's vision. Still, something remained obscure; he felt there should have been more to his experience than just looking at metal shapes and how they were joined together, though he didn't know what.

He skims through the inside pages – the ads, the gossip, the human-interest fillers. Forty-six years after it was posted, a letter is delivered to a woman in a house in the suburbs of a small town in Canada. A love letter, of course; otherwise he wouldn't be reading about it. The woman remembers the man who wrote the letter – he was a soldier; her parents disapproved – and a local reporter has done some reseach. The man is dead, killed a decade ago in a car accident. Driving too fast, double the speed limit, he skidded and smashed into a tree. He was running late.

When holes start appearing in the page in front of him and slowly expanding, like small burns, in places joining up to make larger holes, he screws up his eyes and blinks rapidly. When he looks back, the page is whole again. The words have returned to their places.

The bus is stuck in gridlocked traffic. He should have set off earlier: he has just twenty minutes to get to his hospital appointment. From his window seat on the upper deck – at heart he is six years old or sixteen at most and he likes to be up high and look into people's rooms and lives – he sees a woman in her twenties, blonde, slim, her legs are lovely but her shoes are just wrong, wearing a green dress whose hem isn't cut off straight but folded under and up, and there's something like an air pocket that keeps the whole thing gently afloat – there's technical word for this dress, a fashion word, there must be – *puffball*? – the very dress he once bought for Alicia.

A beach at midday near Genoa: hot light, turquoise, the lazy angles of the bronzing bodies, legs, elbows, breasts, knees.

A flickering neon sign outside a bar glimpsed from the bus back into town.

He is tired, out of sync with the regular tick-tock of the world, and in the gap between himself and what is around him little epiphanies have space to flower, little inklings that all will be well, space to flower and then of course wither because he hasn't the energy to pin them down, to hold them to account. This happens too when he's had two or three glasses of wine, his mind working faster at these times than the ambient tick-tock but again out of sync: all will be well.

When he first saw the holes – but he had no reason then to know then he'd ever see them again – he at once associated them with his father, who was a heavy smoker. He was looking up at a building, a hospital, that was painted a creamy yellow, when holes began to appear in the façade. They were like the holes that appear in a sheet of paper when a cigarette drips hot ash, or is left smouldering on top of it. The edges blacken. They were like what you used to see on the screen when a reel of film stuck in the projector and overheated and began to burn. He is old enough to remember that, when much of the world arrived in black and white. You could smoke in cinemas then, and on the top deck of buses.

A brief cacophony of car horns makes him think there's a wedding, or that Arsenal have finally won the FA Cup, but the traffic is still at a standstill. Usually he has a book, but this morning he slept past the alarm and was rushed and though he thinks he has the book with him he doesn't. It becomes intolerable. He climbs down to the lower deck and stands by the door, waiting for it to open. It won't, until the bus reaches the next stop. Health and safety. He feels a stabbing pain in his left hip. A large woman encumbered with shopping bags offers him her seat. He shakes his head.

The person who told him, only a week ago or maybe two, that London was dirty and inefficient and unfriendly but you get charged £3 for a cup of coffee so smile, you must be living in a major European capital city, could easily have been Alicia. She'd have said it without irony. She didn't have an ounce of irony in her body. She liked living here. She liked, as far as he could tell, living here with him. She didn't live with him for long.

The driver relents, the door wheezes open. Long enough for her hair to lose its absolute blondeness under the grey skies, to darken a shade.

The woman in Canada, now aged seventy-three and living alone, stoops to pick up the post from the doormat – coupons, bills, she hardly ever gets real letters – then sits down at the kitchen table and reads the letter that had taken forty-six years to arrive. She too needs glasses for reading. Then she takes them off and looks out of the window, thinking of her grandchildren who later in the day will be visiting. What shall they do? They will bake scones, she decides. She has the recipe by heart. Winter this year has dragged on and the fields are still covered by snow.

When the black dog came along, the dog others might try to smother with with food, alcohol, indiscriminate sex, retail therapy, Alicia cast off, she slipstreamed. Hence the abandoned puffball dress, now being worn by a stranger.

Soon she will have nothing left to stand up in. Others things too: books, knick-knacks, everything she could carry or throw, all her worldly goods. *It is easier for a camel to pass through the eye of a needle, than for a rich man to enter into the kingdom of God.*

Translators: the back-room boys and girls, the orderlies, the ones in green who wheel the trolleys down the corridors or the ones in white who do the forensics, but who nevertheless are left carrying the can for sins of omission, sins of commission, that were in the original. The assembly instructions tell you to secure the spring-loaded closing mechanism to the overhead flange, but when you look up there is no such flange and never has been. You fudge. You delete or rewrite so that it all joins up. Tiny calculations are involved, all the way along.

Not that she was rich. Once, while travelling, before London, somewhere hot and cheap, he woke in mid-afternoon to her yelp of pain – a splinter had pierced the web of skin between thumb and forefinger, a splinter from a floorboard she was prising up with a blunt knife. He found a screwdriver and helped her. The cracks between the boards were irregular and not caulked. It wasn't hard. They were doing this because they hadn't eaten for two days. Under the floorboards they found enough coins and even banknotes to eat, re-stock, keep going.

Dr Siddique, who has seen it all before, another person who knows more than he does about what is going on, and perhaps it's better this way, is going to tell him that they are planning to slice him open and then stitch him back together again. Women's work. Good Dr Siddique, who always has time to ask him about the book he has with him. There have been days on which, getting ready to set off for the hospital, he has dithered over which book to take, choosing more for her than for himself.

Not that Alicia ever seemed much bothered about the kingdom of God. Not that she wasn't trusting.

There are sirens, police or ambulance, and in between the sirens he can hear a voice declaiming. *At last*, he thinks: war has been declared. The cuts, the *markets in turmoil*, the evil bankers – he agrees, of course, not that anyone has asked him. Someone treads on his foot. The frame of a placard hits his forehead. He raises his hand to the spot and his fingers touch wetness.

'Blotches,' he told Dr Siddique when she asked him to describe the holes. Like the liver spots on the backs of his hands. She looked at him as if expecting him to say more, but there was nothing to add. It wasn't her field; she wanted him to see an eye specialist, but if it's only now and then and he can cure it by blinking, let it be.

He looks up: the sky with its shifting clouds, the office blocks pasted over it. Just as money, above a certain number of zeros, has no reality, so too these buildings: glass, air, fantasy. But not *nothing*.

The sculptor was well known, his work sold for vast sums money, he was interviewed in the papers and appeared on TV. He phoned Alicia. 'Give me a break,' she said, a phrase which sounded wrong in every possible way. But he phoned again, because he wanted know: if the sculptor had been one thing but not the other – rich but not an artist, or an artist but not rich – would she have gone?

'My late girlfriend,' he once said, in the way a widow might say 'my late husband' or a journalist 'the late president'. The man he was talking to gave him a look. He has given those looks himself to people he's known for years but who suddenly give him pause to wonder if he'd trust them with, for example, and if he had one, his wife. Now he is late himself, but perhaps not too late. He will get there and he'll go straight to the lift and rise through the building and walk down the corridor past the trolleys on their rubber wheels and the blank-eyed porters so deep into overtime that neither early nor late has any meaning at all and there she'll be, Alicia – who, having cast off all her worldly belongings, having fasted to the point where her ribs are showing through and her legs can't hold her upright, having almost lost her sight, is now on life support in intensive care, breathing through cloudy tubes in a high white room from whose window you can see the whole of the city, if the weather is fine.

What, Dr Siddique was curious to know, was *in* the holes, or on the other side? Nothing, he said. It's what holes are. You sneeze, you blink, you take your eye off the road, is all it takes. The splinter had pierced right through the web of skin but there was almost no blood, barely a fleck.

No Sharps reads the label on the yellow disposal bin. The luminous green figures on the black monitor flicker and die, flicker and die. The starched sheets that cover her are a landscape that reforms when she turns, when she tries to raise herself up after sleeping, knowing she has a visitor. In Canada snow is still lying in the fields.

The face of the man standing over him, sandy-haired, is the face of his father, his father who was never late in his life. A hole appears in his father's cheek, then another, and though he tries to blink he finds that he can't. It's a mistake, he wants to say. It is easier for a *rope* to pass through the eye of a needle, than for a rich man to enter into the kingdom of God – the camel a mistranslation, the Hebrew was 'rope', and now the only reason people remember it is that someone got it wrong.

THE RAINY SEASON

She worked in an art gallery. It wasn't a good job, meaning neither did it pay well nor did it help to make the world a better place, but it was a harmless one, more harmless even than his own, in the lettings department of an estate agent's. Did this render them safe? They didn't shut their eyes to harm. Maria liked to have the TV switched on all the time, a constant grind of injustice and unreason and hilarity – to know that she wasn't alone, to know that *they* were not alone. The game-show prizes she could take or leave, but someone had to win them.

She worked in an art gallery. And on a Tuesday in February – the week the rain began, the rain that would rain until all records were broken – she was sitting behind her desk, doing whatever she did – Michael still has no idea, the desk was minimalist – when she noticed a visitor on the far side of the gallery. And then what? He stood in front of one of the paintings, he took off his coat and slung it over his shoulder, he turned towards Maria and smiled and Maria recognised her father, who had been dead for ten years.

'You didn't see me come in,' her father said. He was leaning stiffly on a walking stick. It was a criticism, and Maria wasn't used to criticism. She was perfect for the job, everyone had said so: the gallery owner, her sister, friends, Michael too. And then this small matter of resurrection.

'Though I could hardly have walked off with one of these in my pocket,' her father continued. His hair was plastered down by the rain. The smallest of the paintings in the gallery on that wet afternoon was around six foot high. They were paintings of women, and of women with men, in some kind of early-hours, post-party location, and they were so new that the paint was barely dry. Maria had thought they were exciting.

'They're expensive,' Maria said. Her father didn't look rich. Her father looked as if he might ask her for the price of a cup of tea.

'How much?'

'Out of your range.'

'Come on, show me the list.'

The prices started at several thousand pounds.

'Are they a good investment?' the man asked.

'Is that what you think they're for?'

He laughed. 'You're supposed to say yes. You're supposed to sell them to me.'

'Go away,' Maria said. She said that.

Rainwater dripped off his cheap coat and onto the floor. He had always hated water. Maria locked the entrance door and they moved to the office part of the gallery and they sat among the shiny surfaces, the screens and glossy catalogues, and talked. Her father asked if he could smoke and Maria said no. He placed his hands on his knees, a way of sitting that had always made her anxious: it was as if he was about to stand up and leave, as if he had other places to be.

'Are you married?' the man asked her. 'Are you pregnant?'

He read the answers off her face.

~

A week later, she's gone. Michael comes home from work to find an envelope on the kitchen table addressed to himself in her handwriting – her *fluent* handwriting, as if she wrote letters every day or drafts of essays in longhand, even though the only time Michael can remember seeing Maria with a pen in her hand is at Christmas, when she writes a few cards. Does she keep a diary in which she writes about her days and her feelings and himself? He opens the envelope. She loves him, she writes. But she needs to spend some time with her father. She has gone to her sister's, where her father is staying, where there's more room. Her name at the end is a sudden but perfectly legible gust that blows in his face.

That evening, the first time alone in bed for longer than he wants to remember, Michael sleeps badly. He dreams that the police are stopping cars at random on the ring-road, asking to see papers, proof of identity. It's early evening; the police are wearing yellow waterproof capes and the cars' headlights are mirrored on the surface of the wet road. In the centre of town Michael has been photographing children all day, which is not as easy as it sounds: they move quickly, they're here and then they're not here, sometimes tourists step in front of them or a bus passes between the children and Michael and then they are gone. The noise in a city playground that bounces between the walls of the surrounding buildings, this is what Michael really wants to photograph, but he doesn't have the skill. He has been photographing children not because they are innocent (that is not his call), but because they do not deserve to die. He doubts that his accusers will find this a convincing reason. Very soon he expects to be arrested. He will go along without a struggle. The electrodes, the pincers, the thumbscrew, all these can be left in the drawer: he is not a brave man, he will tell them everything they want to know.

～

A dry kiss on both cheeks: Susannah greeting Michael at the door of her house. She points towards the kitchen. Susannah, Maria's older sister, is the Queen of Clubs: tight-lipped, disapproving. In direct sunlight her hair shines orange, a chemical glow. Maria's hair is black and long and fine; she flicks it away from her eyes. No one, seeing Susannah and Maria side by side, would know them to be sisters. For a moment, following Susannah along the hallway, Michael imagines genes as a trembling cascade of motes and flecks in a ray of light, which is not what they are at all.

In semi-darkness, in the glow of a single table light, Maria and a man with white hair are sitting on the kitchen floor, picking up spaghetti from a packet that has split open. Supper will be late. They are picking up the sticks of spaghetti very slowly, and they are taking turns: they are playing a game of pick-a-stick.

Maria's hair is cut short. She has a fringe. She looks ten years younger. She looks like the girl he fell in love with.

The man she calls her father, the man she calls Jules, is asking: 'Do you remember going to the beach and seeing a man parachute out of a plane into the sea? You ran into the water and wouldn't come in when we called.'

And Maria is saying: 'I never heard you!'

'Your mother was shouting –'

'She never shouted –'

'She did when she was angry.'

'I don't remember –'

'You wore a pink bathing costume. Or was it yellow?

'It was pink. It was horrible, prickly . . .'

The pile of spaghetti beside Jules is larger than Maria's pile. Michael, watching from the doorway, thinks Maria is deliberately making mistakes to let him win.

'I had a yellow dress with red lace on the cuffs that was coming away,' Maria says. 'What happened to that dress?'

'What did happen to that dress?'

Jules goes on a run, picking up maybe ten spaghetti sticks one after the other without dislodging any of the others. It occurs to Michael that Jules is training Maria to be a pickpocket. She will be good at this. She moves quickly and can put on a look of absolute innocence. She will work the crowd and bring home her trophies in the evening. He can retire early.

'It moved! That one!'

Maria's turn. 'You know I always wanted a dog,' she says. Concentrating, inching a spaghetti stick from close to the bottom of the pile, she has a focused, interior expression on her face that Michael has always believed he could spend the rest of his life watching and never tire of.

Then Jules makes a daring move. 'We did have a dog,' he says. 'Not for long.'

'What was its name?'

'You don't remember its name?'

'Did he sleep on my bed?

'She. It was a she. Your mother wouldn't have it. All that slobber –'

'Fleas –'

'A labrador. She would wander off for days.'

Maria never had a dog, Michael is sure of this: women don't tell all but they do at some point talk about their childhood pets. He switches on the overhead light and walks into the room, intending to help Maria to her feet, but as he leans towards her he trips over, or is tripped by, Jules's walking stick and falls on top of him. Jules cries out. Michael too is in pain, having bashed his shin against the table as he stumbled. Maria asks him to leave. He knows she is doing this from how she is looking at him, but she says it too.

Susannah is waiting for him by the front door. 'And there's no point phoning,' she tells him. 'She's not answering. Even when I'm out. House rules.'

'Set by who?'

'Who do you think, Michael? The mother of your child.'

Michael looks up at the ceiling. At the angle of the wall with the ceiling there is a cornice, its scrollwork overlayered by decades of repainting, and on the ceiling itself there are brown splashes. How is it possible to spill coffee on a ceiling? Out of nowhere he smells Maria's hair, a smell he could drown in.

'And no emails,' Susannah adds. 'She's in purdah.'

'For him too?'

'Not for him. Actually he's not so bad. He helps around, he does the washing-up.'

'A man with a walking stick does the washing-up?'

'He's not a cripple.'

'I thought he hated water.'

'People change, Michael.'

≈

There are squalls and showers; there are periods of persistent, accumulative drizzle; there is, mostly, the kind of rain that is so light you can't see that it's there, you can only feel it on your skin like a veil.

Jules is standing outside the front door, smoking, which he isn't allowed to do inside. He likes smoking more than he dislikes the rain. Can you hit a man who is smoking? A man who is not just smoking but who is smaller than you, and older, and lame?

The true Jules walked out of his family's life when Maria was a child. He lived abroad and there was no communication until Maria's mother received an envelope from Italy that looked like a tax demand, so it gathered dust on the mantelpiece for at least a month until Maria herself opened it. She knew enough Italian, anyone does, to understand the word *morto*.

None of this was news to Maria's mother, who had known for years that her husband was dead – drowned, in a river below a waterfall. He had never learned to swim. The document from Italy stated that he had died in a street in Rome after being hit by a reversing truck, but Maria's mother knew otherwise: she had been with him in the river, tumbling down. She wrote a courteous letter – a *thank-you* letter – to the Italian lawyer, or coroner, from whose office the envelope had arrived; and then, realising that she hadn't after all drowned beneath the waterfall, that her lungs still drew breath, she rang the numbers in an old address book, crossing out the names of those who were dead or who struggled for too long to remember who she was. She joined a beginners' class in Spanish, she asked advice about hairdressers. She went shopping, and was relieved to find that almost everything she could be spending her money on she didn't really want. What *did* she want? On the third floor of John Lewis in Oxford Street things began to swim out of focus and she felt her legs giving way beneath her. The man who picked her up, who sat her in a chair and spoke to her respectfully, patiently, had such a kind voice she wanted him to do it all over again. Instead he put her in a taxi. *I'll be fine, thank you, I'll be fine*, she told him, but not too convincingly because the next day he phoned her to make sure. He was a Scottish solicitor named Ray, and when he suggested dinner she had the good sense or recklessness to say yes.

'How is Maria?' Michael asks the false Jules.

Maria is doing fine. She's been for a scan, she's stopped work early, she is happy.

'I want to see her.' And then, seeing Jules isn't going to budge, 'Can you give her this?' – a carrier bag containing grapes, underwear and a letter of fourteen pages in Michael's own crabbed, inelegant handwriting.

Jules takes the bag and offers Michael a cigarette. Michael declines, he doesn't smoke, and he asks Jules what, since he died, he's been up to. It's like interviewing someone with an unexplained gap in their c.v.

∾

Michael has nothing to argue from, just a single photograph of a man wearing a crumpled suit standing beside a picnic table in the snow, with a woman's scarf tied around his head. The building in the background, behind a stand of trees, looked vaguely like a hotel, but Maria had no idea where the photograph was taken. Her father travelled around a lot, to conferences and galleries and the hideaway homes of aged and reclusive artists. What did they talk about, these artists and her father, these artists whom most people assumed were dead? Who was the woman whose scarf was around his head? As for why he was wearing it, either it was because of the cold or he had earache. He looked like a child who has been sent out to play by himself while the grown-ups sit round a table and talk about grown-up things.

Old-style parenting, before parenting was even a verb.

The new Jules too is a child, even though he has whitish, in places yellowish, hair, swept back, with little tufts at the ends and around the ears. Weatherbeaten, or he's a drinker. Nicotine-stained teeth and fingers. Very pale eyes. His walking stick is his favourite toy, his comfort blanket. Is this a man, Michael asks himself, whose genes he'd be happy to see given another run-out? Is this a man he'd even be happy to let a run-down studio flat to?

On a day in April Michael is standing under a large yellow umbrella that bears the logo of the estate agent he works for and his shoes are leaking and he has been waiting outside a block of mansion flats for forty minutes. The tenth car that passes by will be his client, looking for a parking space. The client, he imagines, will be Maria, and in the vacant flat on the hard bed beneath the spreading patch of damp in the room with a view over a supermarket delivery bay they will slowly undress each other and make love. The next tenth car . . . The client, he imagines, will be Jules, thrown out by Susannah and needing somewhere to go to ground: if Jules is not Maria's father he is a chancer, a loner, on the run from someone or something, from consequences he didn't foresee. If you pass him in the street you don't lock eyes. He is one of those of those people the police warn the public not to approach.

Back in the office – after a hundred and twenty cars and still no client – his line manager asks to see him. The weather, his line manager explains. No house looks good in the rain. People feel trapped; they stay indoors, they stop moving around. A downturn in the market, and Michael is being *let go*.

While Michael is clearing his desk his colleague Derek is looking at girls in bikinis on his screen; next up are palm-fringed beaches and columns of prices for self-catering bungalows with/without private swimming pools in Guadeloupe. Some people get cold and wet, other people get skin cancer. Michael wishes Derek happy times on his holiday, and leaves. 'Goodbye, Mike,' says Derek, his eyes still on the screen.

On his way home, Michael passes by the gallery where Maria no longer works. There are waterlogged brown squares on the walls, something heavy and ecological but yielding the odd bone or trinket, and a new girl at the desk: younger, cheaper. Fathers too, Michael understands, after they've done their biological bit, are dispensable, redundant. What's left is ageing: carving the joint on Sundays, making paper hats out of yesterday's newspapers. They are a drain on resources. Not so very long until he too will be hard of hearing, deaf to the *beep-beep* of a reversing truck.

∼

Jules at Susannah's front door again: except for the smoking, like a sentry at Buckingham Palace.

Back in the early days, relaxed after wine and/or making love, Maria recalled for Michael not her former lovers but the several candidates she had asked to take over the job of father, the job that Jules had quit. The first, her school chaplain: how could he say no? He had thinning hair and spoke with a soft reasonableness that stilled all doubt, however far-fetched the matter in the books he had to read aloud from. Our Father, he said at morning assembly, and the children all bowed their heads but Maria kept her eyes tilted upwards and he knew she was watching him, she was sure of that. The school prospectus already had him down as spiritual counsellor: it just needed a slight push. One afternoon she found him alone in his classroom, marking books. 'I don't think you really mean that,' he said, and she thought that someone had perhaps asked him before and then it had turned out they were making a joke or doing it for a dare. 'You don't have to decide right now,' she said, and he moved his chair to one side as if he was about to ask her to sit next to him so they could work out sensibly what happened next, but at the same time he looked back at the exercise book he was marking and she knew then that she was doomed. And so was he. And so, judging by his scribbles in the margins, was the child who had written the homework.

Jules is listening as Michael talks. Again he proffers his cigarettes.

Michael takes one.

She went through a phase of favouring loners, men on the fringes whose view of others coincided, she rashly assumed, with hers. Most looked away; a few of them didn't. Mr X – she didn't know his name at the time – was often on the same bus as Maria and her sister on their way to school. He had eyes set so far back you couldn't tell what he was looking at. Then he was in the park too, in summer, sitting on a bench, still with his raincoat on, and one afternoon Maria sat down next to him and spoke. He was never seen on the bus or in the park again. Once or twice in the local shops – head down, counting his change. He moved to Wales. Maria knew this because some years later he sent her a Christmas card.

'So how did she end up with *you*?' Jules asks Michael. 'What made her change the job description?'

Inside the house the telephone rings. Susannah is out. A wrong number, Michael thinks; or the right number but whoever is ringing will stay silent. This is a ghost story of sorts.

~

Maria is back! – stumbling out of a taxi, her hair wet with rain, her cheeks wet with tears. She has quarrelled with Jules, and with Susannah too, and Michael enfolds her, kisses her, and she responds, and he takes her – *carries* her – into the flat. She is tired but doesn't want to sleep, or she wants to sleep but isn't tired. She doesn't know: whether Jules is her father, whether she wants to be here or back at Susannah's, whether she wants to be a mother or it's all a terrible mistake. She wants to be here, Michael decides for her. He runs a hot bath and undresses her – this familiar, unfamiliar body – and bathes her and puts her to bed, and after watching until she is asleep he goes into the living room and falls fitfully asleep himself on the sofa. He dreams that he is sitting at a table with Maria in a fisherman's hut with a corrugated-iron roof, and the rain drumming on the roof is so loud that he can't hear what Maria is saying. There are fish scales glistening on the wooden floor. He leans close, feels her breath on his face. She is saying how at times like these, in places like these – and, obviously, in crowded bars – it would help if everyone could talk in speech bubbles that come out of their mouths, so people can read each other's speech rather than having to struggle to hear it. It's quite dark, Michael points out. But the bubbles could be illuminated from within.

When he wakes it's still early, before seven, and in the bedroom the bed is empty and unslept-in.

He phones Susannah and arranges to meet her in a bar, but at nine o'clock that evening either she has forgotten or he is in the wrong bar and a woman who is neither Susannah nor Maria is leaning across the table to inspect Michael's eyebrows, eyes, the texture of the skin on his cheeks. She puts a finger on his chin and he opens his mouth. Wider. She peers inside. Upper left three, filling coming loose. Lower right six – where did that one go? 'Really, no one in Norway has teeth like these. You should see –'

'I know, I know. I've been told.'

She says that his teeth are a disaster, a catastrophe. Michael thinks she is exaggerating. Her name is Birgit and she is a dental nurse.

'They didn't have the treatments, the alloys, in those days,' he says, knowing this is hardly an excuse that will stand up in court. He wonders if, now that he is unemployed, he can get dental treatment for free, along with the children and the pregnant women.

'What does *enamelled* mean?'

Her English is good but not perfect. He says it means something has a hard surface, to protect it. Cars, for example: they use enamel paint. Coffee pots. People. '*Teeth* have enamel.'

'But very thin. Enamel gets worn away,' she says.

She shifts in her seat and takes a book from her bag. She searches for a page and again reaches across the table, her finger pointing halfway down the page.

Michael reads: 'James was enamoured of Alice.'

'Oh, *enamoured*,' he says. 'It means love. James loves Alice. He fancies her.'

'Are you enamoured of Maria?' Her freckles are all bunched up.

'Yes, I am enamoured of Maria.' He drinks from his beer. 'You can be enamoured of more than one person,' he adds.

'How many? Ten, twenty?'

'That's spreading it a bit thin.'

She looks puzzled. Her clear blue eyes, constellation of freckles. Icy fjords.

∾

Michael conjugates: I rain, you rain, he-she-or-it rains. He watches a puddle expand to the point of touching another puddle, and welcome it, and pool again into another. He is a patient man.

In May Jules finds himself a job. A dust sheet has been laid in Susannah's hallway and Jules is on a ladder with a tiny mallet and a chisel, chipping out layers of paint from the ceiling cornice to expose the original detail. Why now,

Michael wonders – why now, after generations of benign neglect, and why by a man in his sixties who's unsteady on a ladder? Does looking up to the man make Jules a role model?

Jules has been working, he says, for two days, and has cleaned out a stretch no longer than a foot. He too is a patient man. To finish the whole hallway will take him until the unborn child is in secondary school.

Flakes of yellowed paint decorate Jules's hair like dandruff. Old paint was made with lead, wasn't it? The dust can be carcinogenic, Michael recalls reading somewhere. He asks Jules if this if this is a good thing to be doing, if the dust could be harmful to Maria. Jules pretends not to hear him. He drops the mallet, which Michael hands back. The brown splashes are still there on the ceiling.

Two weeks later there is a rearrangement prompted, Michael guesses, by Susannah's impatience with Jules's refusal to quit smoking. Jules moves into the garage which adjoins the house. Gardening forks, trowels and shears hang from nails, rusting. At the back, over a workbench, the door of a kitchen cabinet has fallen off; inside are ancient jam-jars, bottles of weedkiller, plant pots. There are cobwebs with mummified flies. Michael thinks: a man could hang himself in here. Jules has a sleeping bag laid over a flattened cardboard box; two folding garden chairs are set up on the concrete floor

'Have you read *Anna Karenina*?' Jules asks.

Michael has seen the film, he thinks, or a TV adaptation. 'Have *you* read it?'

'I read it a long time ago,' Jules says. 'When everyone was much younger – Kitty, Levin, Vronsky, all of them. It has recipes for making jam.'

Beautiful and intelligent and rich, all of these people,

with country estates and nothing to do during the long fine days except talk and make jam, and Michael resents them: safe, between the covers of a book.

'How old were you? And those other people?'

'Your age, maybe. What are you reading now?'

Michael is reading, on and off, *The Rough Guide to Pregnancy and Childbirth*, an innocent's guide to a foreign land of which he, as a mere tourist, will never be granted citizenship. On the other hand, nor will he be conscripted for national service or have to pay the sky-high taxes.

Jules finds a wooden crate on top of the cabinet with the broken door, and they place the crate between the chairs and they play cards. Sometimes Maria joins them. They play Black Jack, which Maria remembers playing as a child, and Jules remembers the game too but they disagree over the rules. Can you play immediately after you've picked up, or do you have to wait until your next turn? Jules lets Maria decide. She is looking healthy and strong but her hair, which she has started to grow long again, is dry and straggly. She smells different – a ripeness, new undercurrents. In the womb, nerve cells are being formed in the child's brain at a rate of 10,000 per second – half die off, because they don't make connections with other cells. You have to wait until your next turn, she decides. Michael kneels in front of her and kisses her belly, round and swollen and taut but still yielding, neither solid nor liquid. *Amniotic*: he can't get the word out his head. He breathes it into her ear; he feels that he himself is floating, adrift. Jules has fallen asleep in his garden chair, his walking stick on the ground beside him. Every now and then Michael is sure he can hear, not far distant, a child crying, wanting its something.

'Is there someone else?' Maria asks him.

Of course there is someone else, he wants to tell her.

There is always someone else: even if they are only Derek, even if they have gone away or haven't yet arrived.

Sometimes when Michael switches on the radio in the flat he finds it tuned to strange effervescent stations. The television, which weeks ago Michael threw a rug over – what does it *mean*, to be told that there is a depression moving in from the west? – is now uncovered and back on: for her English, Birgit says. In Devon and the Lake District there are floods: the news shows fields under sheets of water, bridges washed away, canoes in the high streets. The floodwater is the brown of diluted mud and excrement. Michael sits down and watches, fascinated, as helicopters winch families to safety from their rooftops, the women and children first, as on the *Titanic*, the elderly also a favoured category.

In bra and pants, Birgit does exercises in Michael's bedroom. Not as deliberate as yoga, not a full work-out either; something Norwegian.

'Do you want to go swimming?' he asks her.

She has a life-guard's certificate. She is a water nymph.

'You know,' she says, 'you close your eyes when you make love.'

'Do I?'

'Do I close my eyes too?'

'How would I know, if my eyes are closed?'

'Maybe you peek when I'm not looking.'

The army is helping out. The death toll is rising. The prime minister is coming under pressure to declare a state of emergency, as if that will change anything.

∾

The sky is the colour of rain. The rain is the colour of the sky.

A drawer beneath the bench at the back of the garage is stuck. Michael tugs and then rattles it, and finally it springs open. Inside the drawer are small cardboard boxes; once upon a time the half-inch nails kept to one box and the three-quarter ones to another and the staples to another and so on, but now everything is commingling, cohabiting.

He remembers those children's picture books – there must be one still in the house, among the too many things, on a shelf that has gathered dust – whose pages are divided into three parts that you turn separately, and so construct a tripartite animal with the head of an owl, the body of a rabbit and the feet of a duck.

There is a day when Michael goes shopping for new shoes, shoes that will not leak, and in the mall he goes for a coffee. The shopping mall is *dry*: it is another condition of being, it is like being asleep or on holiday. Everything around him is bright and shiny and new; everything except the air, which is being continuously recycled.

A man with a limp and downcast eyes, unconvinced of the value of what's he's selling, approaches Michael and offers him a leaflet – as many as he wants – promising that Jesus Saves. Michael ignores him, but the man persists. Michael makes a gesture with his hands to indicate he hasn't got any money, or that today he's not interested in being saved (maybe tomorrow, maybe next week), then looks at the man and sees that it is Jules, and his teeth are even worse than his own.

'How is the Norwegian?' Jules asks.

'She's only here a few months. To learn how we do things in this country.'

'Oral hygiene.'

'She's an exchange student. She's leaving soon.'

'In exchange for someone else?'

'The student who's coming back from Norway.'

'I didn't mean that.'

'Where's your walking stick?' Michael asks.

As if remembering that he has difficulty in standing up unaided, Jules puts his leaflets on the table and slumps into the seat next to Michael. A woman walks past, hunched down, like a miscarriage of justice. Michael thinks: why doesn't Jules offer his leaflets to *her*? Meanwhile, the water table is rising. One day soon the ground around him, this shopping mall included, will be marshland, home to all manner of waders and aquatic insects. As it used to be, only so many generations before.

~

In late summer Michael has a dream in which he *almost* makes love with Maria, several times. (In the pregnancy book, there is no entry in the index for dreams; he has looked.) He is in a hotel with deep-pile beige carpets and brass ashtrays on stands along the corridors, or he is in some dictator's palace with secret passages and torture chambers, and every so often he finds himself alone with Maria and comes very close, close enough for touching and unbuttoning, before other people arrive and they have to rush off elsewhere. One of the other people is Derek. Another is Birgit but it's Maria he wants now. The touch of her, the juice of her. The juice of her what? Damn this dream, he says to himself inside the dream, but there is Maria again and surely *this* time . . . He wakes up.

It is 4 a.m. and a thunderstorm is raging overhead – what has woken Michael is the sound of rain pounding on the roof. Except that the flat is on the first floor and doesn't have a roof, and when Michael goes to the window he sees that it isn't raining at all. The pounding noise is that of a thousand feet – more, far more – tramping the road below: an unbroken stream of runners in shorts and vests coming up the hill and past the block of flats and, as far as Michael can see, turning left at the traffic lights. An undercover marathon.

Michael puts on a coat and stands out on the balcony. For the past months he has been married to the rain. In its absence he feels light, empty, transparent. If he jumped he would fly. Some of the runners look up and wave. He waves back, like shy royalty.

The sky is damp and dark but the whole scene is lit with a neon glow that makes every detail clear, and with a shiver that has nothing to with the cold Michael recognises the runners: every one of them is male and every one of them is Jules. There are boys as young as ten who are already Jules and there are old men with stringy legs who are *still* Jules, and there are those who have smoked too many cigarettes for too many years and the fat ones who are in danger of collapsing and who should never have even signed up but who are kept going by a demented team spirit, a stubborn refusal to let the side down.

Either that, or else they have already had their coronaries and their liver diseases and car crashes and freak accidents, so that what in fact Michael is witnessing is a parade of the dead.

Where is the finishing line? Or is the route a continuous loop?

After around half an hour, when the continuous mass has thinned out to isolated stragglers and the occasional Jules in a wheelchair, his arms pumping against the slope of the hill, it starts to rain, real rain this time, and Michael goes inside, runs a hot bath, makes coffee and phones Susannah.

~

By noon the next day Michael and Maria are in a hired car driving north to visit Maria's mother, who is ill. Maria's voice comes from behind him; her seat is tilted back as far as it will go, their child in her body rising beside him.

'Sometimes my father would come into my room to check if I was asleep, late at night, and I'd hear his footsteps coming and pretend to be asleep. And sometimes he'd sit for a while on the end of my bed, watching me.' She laughs. She might have never been away. 'I suppose that's what he was doing. I kept my eyes tight closed. I was terrified.'

'I thought he wasn't at home much,' Michael says.

'But when he was.'

'Why didn't you open your eyes?'

'I was frightened. I was frightened from the moment I heard his footsteps on the stairs, from when I began *waiting* for his footsteps on the stairs. I couldn't go to sleep until it was all over.'

'Frightened of what?'

'That it wasn't him. That it was someone else.'

'Who?'

She does a *pffft* with her lips, then smiles dreamily. 'Those nights,' she says. 'High point of my life.'

Tonight they will stay in a cheap hotel in Edinburgh where the heating cannot be turned down and the window cannot be opened; Highland cattle will stand guard on the walls.

'You know that scene in a movie where the walls start moving inwards?' Maria says. 'What was the name of that film?'

Maria's mother is not ill, Michael thinks, not in the way she used to be when she believed that her husband had drowned. (And then, when the news of his actual death arrived from Italy, she had wanted to frame the certificate and hang it on the wall. Susannah had said no; it wasn't a *qualification*, not like the certificates on the walls of cafés and dentists' waiting rooms.) She is normal, now. She has a mild cold, and she wants to be visited. She will run down the steps to greet Maria and Michael with an actressy glee; she will do her level best to get them on speaking terms with the American couple who also happen to be staying for the weekend, who are old friends of Ray and whom Michael will dislike at first sight. She will pull out all the stops. There will be clean maroon towels in the en-suite bathroom.

Michael asks: 'Do you do that with me?'

'Do what?'

The times he has watched her sleeping – when he comes home late, after she has gone to bed; when he wakes in the pre-dawn light.

'Oh,' she says, 'you mean, do I pretend? Pretend I'm asleep? No. Why should I?'

'I thought everyone did.'

She doesn't answer.

'I do,' he says. 'When you get up for a pee –'

'If *you* were pregnant –'

'And I'm awake but I keep my eyes closed, so that when you come back –'

'Yes, that's nice. Getting back into bed.'

'Chilled, like something from the fridge –'

'On a hot day –'

'First touch. Delicious.'

'Second touch?'

She takes his left hand from the steering wheel and places it on her forehead. 'Every night,' she says, 'just before he left, he'd stroke my brow. Very gently.'

'He or the someone else.'

'A kind of signal – he was about to go, and after that I could stop pretending.'

'And open your eyes.'

'No one there at all.'

He moves his hand across to the dome of her belly, listening through his fingers for the gloop and slurp of sea-born creatures before their fins become limbs and they struggle on to land, then brings it back to the steering wheel. Sometimes the shifting pattern of the traffic is forcing him to drive faster than he wants to.

'Any special requests?'

The windscreen wipers sweep left, sweep right, battling the spray thrown up by the traffic in front. Michael sees the bed in the mansion flat beneath the damp stain on the ceiling, the sheets rumpled, needing a wash. He sees the wife of the American man – Doreen, her name is; she has a daughter aged twenty-four who lives in Singapore and a son, slightly retarded, who works in a supermarket just twelve miles away from their home in Connecticut and whom she sees just as seldom – doing the thing with the ring, if Maria doesn't mind, she's always wondered if it really works, tying the ring – does it have to be gold? can it be any ring? – to a piece of string and dangling it over Maria's bump. Is it clockwise for a boy and anticlockwise for a girl or the other way round? Or from side to side? 'Surely *someone* must remember,' Doreen pleads, but no one does, or if they do they're not saying. It doesn't matter anyway. The string with the ring stays obstinately vertical. Michael suggests that someone should blow it, to give it a start, like cranking up a car's engine in olden times, but that isn't allowed.

It's a boy, it has to be, because of the whole father thing. Or else a girl.

About half an hour later Maria tells him to drive faster, and if he can't do that she wants to stop, right now. They are on a motorway; the car is being jolted, rocked, drenched by passing lorries. Through the blizzard of spray, visibility is almost nil. He drives another five miles to the next service station, and even before he has parked the car she is struggling to release the seat belt. 'Let me out,' she says.

ACKNOWLEDGEMENTS

ACKNOWLEDGEMENTS

'Budapest' was first printed in *The Warwick Review* (March 2012). 'Distraction' was published online in *3:AM*, and 'The Rainy Season' in the online journal *The Long Story, Short*.